From the desk of Emerald Larson, owner and CEO of Emerald, Inc.

To: My personal assistant, Luther Freemont

Re: My newly discovered grandson, Nick Daniels

My grandson, Nick, will be leaving at the end of the week to take over running the Sugar Creek Cattle Company in Wyoming. Please be advised that he won't be particularly happy when he discovers that his ranch foreman is the woman he was to have married thirteen years ago. To ensure the success of my plan and avoid the fallout of his displeasure, I am instructing you to intercept all calls from him until further notice.

As always, I am relying on your complete discretion in this matter.

Emerald Larson

Silhouette Desire is proud to present an exciting new miniseries from

KATHIE DENOSKY

The Illegitimate Heirs

In January 2006—
ENGAGEMENT BETWEEN ENEMIES

In February 2006—
REUNION OF REVENGE

In March 2006—
BETROTHED FOR THE BABY

Dear Reader,

It's February and that means Cupid is ready to shoot his arrow into the hearts of the six couples in this month's Silhouette Desire novels. The first to get struck by love is Teagan Elliott, hero of Brenda Jackson's *Taking Care of Business,* book two of THE ELLIOTTS continuity. Teagan doesn't have romance on his mind when he meets a knock-out social worker…but when the sparks fly between them there's soon little else he can think of.

In *Tempt Me* by Caroline Cross, Cupid doesn't so much as shoot an arrow as tie this hero up in chains. How he got into this predicament…and how he gets himself out is a story not to be missed in this second MEN OF STEELE title. Revenge, not romance, plays a major role in our next two offerings. Kathie DeNosky's THE ILLEGITIMATE HEIRS trilogy continues with a hero hell-bent on making his position as his old flame's new boss a *Reunion of Revenge.* And in *His Wedding-Night Wager* by Katherine Garbera, the first of a new trilogy called WHAT HAPPENS IN VEGAS…, a jilted groom gets the chance to make his runaway bride pay.

Seven years is a long time for Cupid to do his job, but it looks like he might have finally struck a chord with the stranded couple forced to reexamine their past relationship, in Heidi Betts's *Seven-Year Seduction.* And rounding out the month is a special Valentine's Day delivery by author Emily McKay, who makes her Silhouette Desire debut with *Surrogate and Wife.*

Here's hoping romance strikes you this month as you devour these Silhouette Desire books as fast as a box of chocolate hearts!

Best,

Melissa Jeglinski

Melissa Jeglinski
Senior Editor
Silhouette Desire

Please address questions and book requests to:
Silhouette Reader Service
U.S.: 3010 Walden Ave., P.O. Box 1325, Buffalo, NY 14269
Canadian: P.O. Box 609, Fort Erie, Ont. L2A 5X3

KATHIE DeNOSKY

Reunion
of Revenge

Published by Silhouette Books
America's Publisher of Contemporary Romance

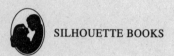

SILHOUETTE BOOKS

ISBN 0-373-76707-2

REUNION OF REVENGE

Copyright © 2006 by Kathie DeNosky

Visit Silhouette Books at www.eHarlequin.com

Printed in U.S.A.

KATHIE DeNOSKY

lives in her native southern Illinois with her husband and one very spoiled Jack Russell terrier. She writes highly sensual stories with a generous amount of humor. Kathie's books have appeared on the Waldenbooks bestseller list and received the Write Touch Readers' Award from WisRWA and the National Readers' Choice Award. Kathie enjoys going to rodeos, traveling to research settings for her books and listening to country music. Readers may contact Kathie at: P.O. Box 2064, Herrin, Illinois 62948-5264 or e-mail her at kathie@kathiedenosky.com.

For Charlie, Bryan, David and Angie,
for loving me in spite of my eccentricities.

From the desk of Emerald Larson, owner and CEO of Emerald, Inc.

To: My personal assistant, Luther Freemont
Re: My grandson Nick Daniels

My grandson, Nick, will be leaving at the end of the week to take over running the Sugar Creek Cattle Company in Wyoming. Please be advised that he won't be particularly happy when he discovers that his ranch foreman is the woman he was to have married thirteen years ago. To ensure the success of my plan and to avoid the fallout of his displeasure, I am instructing you to intercept all calls from him until further notice.

As always I am relying on your complete discretion in this matter.

Emerald Larson

One

"**D**rop that roll of wire and back away from your truck."

Nick Daniels took a deep breath and tried to ignore the jolt of awareness that shot from the top of his head all the way to his feet. It had been thirteen long years since he'd heard that soft, feminine voice. But if he lived to be a hundred, he knew he'd recognize it anywhere, anytime. The melodic sound had haunted his dreams and left his body aching with unfathomable need too many nights for him to ever forget.

"I told you to put that down and step away from the truck."

At the sound of a shotgun being pumped, Nick slowly lowered the coil of barbed wire to the tailgate of his new truck and raised his gloved hands to show he was complying with her command. Then, turning to face the reason he'd left Wyoming one step ahead of the law, he smiled sardonically. "It's been a long time, Cheyenne."

The widening of her eyes and the slight wavering of the double-barrel shotgun she pointed at him were the only indications that she was the least bit surprised to see him after all this time. "I don't know what you think you're doing out here, Nick Daniels, but I'd advise you to get in your truck and go back to wherever you came from. Otherwise, I'll call the law."

He took a deep breath as he stared at her. Damned if she wasn't more beautiful now than she'd been at sixteen. Her long brown hair, streaked with golden highlights, complemented the healthy glow of her sun-kissed skin and her aqua-green eyes to perfection.

His gaze drifted lower. Her pink tank top caressed her torso, fascinating the hell out of him and giving him more than a fair idea about the size and shape of her breasts. He swallowed hard as his gaze drifted even lower. She'd always been a knockout in a pair of jeans, but the well-worn denim hugged her hips and thighs like a second skin and emphasized how long and shapely her legs were.

He diverted his gaze back to the gun in her hands. He'd do well to forget how good she looked after all this time and concentrate on the fact that she was ready to blow his ass to kingdom come.

"Go ahead and call the sheriff. Last time I heard, it wasn't against the law for a man to mend a fence on his own property."

"It's not your land. It belongs to the Sugar Creek Cattle Company. And you're trespassing."

He shook his head as he took a step toward her. "No, I'm not."

"I swear I'll shoot you if you don't stop right there, Nick."

"That wouldn't be very neighborly of you, sweetheart."

"Don't call me that." She released the safety on the shotgun when he moved forward.

From the sharp edge he'd heard in her voice, he knew he'd hit a nerve. He inched a little closer. "You used to like when I called you sweetheart."

She shook her head. "That's past history. Now, get in your truck and disappear like you did thirteen years ago."

"Why would I want to do that? This is my home." With the gun barrel still pointed at the middle of his chest, he wisely chose not to point out that her father had been behind his disappearing act back then, or that he was damned tired of a Holbrook trying to run him off his own land. "If you'll remember, the Sugar Creek ranch has been in my family for over a hundred and twenty-five years."

"If *you'll* remember, you gave up the right to this land a long time ago." Was that bitterness he detected in her voice?

"That's where you're wrong, Cheyenne." Easing forward a bit more, he was almost close enough to reach the shotgun. "I still own this place, lock, stock…" He lunged forward and, grabbing the shotgun, shoved it away with one hand at the same time he reached out to wrap his arm around her waist. "…and barrel," he finished, pulling her to him.

"Turn me loose." She pushed at his chest as she tried to wiggle from his grasp.

"Not until we get a few things straight." The feel of her soft body squirming against his was heaven and hell rolled into one shapely little five-foot-two-inch package. He did his best to ignore it. "When you point a gun at a man, you'd better be prepared to use it, sweetheart."

"I was." She sounded breathless and if he didn't know better, he'd swear he felt a slight tremor pass through her.

Shaking his head as much in answer to her statement as in an attempt to clear his mind, he whispered close to her ear, "You and I both know you could never shoot me, Cheyenne."

"Let me have my gun back…and I'll show you." There was no doubt that she shivered against him this time.

He couldn't resist teasing the side of her neck with his lips. "Not until you calm down."

Her labored breathing quickly reminded him of the changes in her body since the last time he'd held her. At sixteen, Cheyenne Holbrook had had a figure that sent his hormones racing around like the steel bearings in a pinball machine. But that had only been a hint of the woman she would become. Her breasts were fuller now and her hips had a slight flare that promised to cradle a man and take him to paradise when he sank himself deep inside her.

When his lower body tightened, he cursed himself as the biggest fool God ever blessed with the breath of life. He wasn't an eighteen-year-old kid anymore. He was a thirty-one-year-old man and should have mastered at least a modicum of restraint.

"Turn me loose."

When she pushed against him this time, he let her go, but held on to the gun. He shook his head when she reached for it. "I'll hang on to this for a while longer."

"Suit yourself." She reached for the cell phone clipped to her belt. "It's not going to stop me from calling Sheriff Turner and having you arrested for trespassing."

"You do that."

Her finger hovered over the phone's dial pad as she glanced up at him. "You aren't worried about being arrested?"

"Why should I be? I own the Sugar Creek." He shrugged as he placed the shotgun on the tailgate of his truck, well out of her reach. "You, on the other hand, are on my land." He stopped short of adding that her father and the sheriff would have a hell of a time getting him to leave again.

"I don't think so." She impatiently brushed a silky strand of hair from her cheek as she glared at him. "Emerald, Inc. is the corporation that bought your ranch after you and your mother left."

"The hell you say." He removed his leather work gloves, then, tucking them into the waistband of his jeans, he folded his arms across his chest. "And just how would you know that?"

She looked hesitant a moment before taking a deep breath and defiantly looking him square in the eye. "I'm the foreman of the Sugar Creek Cattle Company. Don't you think I'd know who my employer is?"

Nick couldn't believe it. Cheyenne's father, the judge, had actually allowed his precious daughter to work? And at a job where she might actually get her hands dirty? Interesting.

It appeared that Emerald Larson had omitted a couple of important details when she told him she was his grandmother and gave him back the ranch. She'd explained her reasoning behind having his mother sign documents stating that the identity of his father would remain a secret until she deemed he was ready to learn the truth. She'd even solved the mystery of who had tipped his mother off about his impending arrest the night they left Wyoming when she told him that she'd had a private investigator reporting his every move from the time he was born. But she hadn't mentioned anything about Cheyenne Holbrook being the ranch foreman. And as soon as he went back to the house, he was going to call Wichita and find out what other surprises the old gal had in store for him.

"I know this is going to come as a shock to you, but I really am the owner of this spread," Nick said.

Cheyenne paled, then stubbornly shook her head. "I don't believe you. When Luther Freemont from the corporate office called me just last week to discuss my quarterly report, he didn't mention anything about Emerald, Inc. selling the Sugar Creek."

Nick wasn't surprised to hear the name of Emerald's personal assistant. She trusted the man implic-itly and relied on him to be the liaison between her and most of the managers of the companies she owned.

"I'll tell you what, Cheyenne." He picked up the shotgun and emptied the shells from its chamber be-fore handing it to her. Then, pocketing the ammuni-tion, he pointed to the truck she'd parked several yards away. "Why don't you go back to your father's ranch and give old Luther a call?"

"Don't think I won't," she said, raising her stub-born little chin a notch.

"After you hear what he has to say, we'll go from there." Nick pulled his work gloves from the waist-band of his jeans and prepared to finish mending the section of fence he'd thought looked weak before he went back home to call Emerald. "Be over at my house tomorrow morning at nine."

"Why?"

She didn't look at all happy about having to see him again. And he knew as surely as he knew his own name that she didn't for a minute believe he was tell-ing the truth about owning the Sugar Creek.

"We'll have to discuss the terms of your contract." He grinned. "And the last I heard, it's pretty common for a rancher and his foreman to work together run-ning a ranch."

In an obvious test of wills, she glared at him for

several more seconds before turning to stalk back to her truck.

As Nick watched her leave, he couldn't stop himself from noticing the gentle sway of her delightful little backside as she walked away. She still had the ability to take his breath away with her beauty and with no more than a touch she could make him harder than hell in less than two seconds flat.

But he'd do well to remember that her father was the mighty Judge Bertram Holbrook, the most ill-tempered, acrimonious son of a bitch on two legs. A man who had half the county officials in his pocket and the other half scared to death he'd turn his wrath their way.

And if Holbrook had his way about it, Nick would still be rotting away in jail, simply because he'd tried to marry the man's only daughter.

The next morning, as Cheyenne drove the five miles between the Flying H and the Sugar Creek ranch houses, she wondered for at least the hundredth time what she could do about the situation. When she'd talked to Luther Freemont after her confrontation with Nick, she'd developed a splitting headache. He'd confirmed everything Nick had told her and, feeling as if her world had once again been turned completely upside down, she'd ended up lying awake the entire night, reliving the past and worrying about what the future held for her and her father.

It had taken her years to get over the devastation when Nick walked away from their relationship—from her—without so much as a backward glance, and seeing him after all this time had shaken her more than she could have ever imagined. But when he'd grabbed her to take away her gun, she couldn't believe the awareness that coursed through her traitorous body. At the feel of his rock-hard muscles surrounding her, she'd grown warm from the top of her head all the way to her toes and drawing her next breath had taken supreme effort. It had also scared her as little else could.

When they'd been teenagers, she'd thought the sun rose and set around Nick. He'd been two years ahead of her in school and the best-looking boy in the county. With his dark blond hair, charming smile and tall, muscular build, he'd been every sixteen-year-old girl's dream and every father's worst nightmare. Her pulse sped up as she remembered the heart-pounding excitement she'd felt the first time Nick had turned his sky-blue eyes and charming smile her way. She'd instantly fallen head over heels in love.

But her father wouldn't hear of her having anything to do with Nick. He'd told her the boy was nothing but bad news and a heartache waiting to happen. He'd never explained why he felt that way about

Nick, but unfortunately, she'd found out the hard way that her father had been been right.

When he and the sheriff had stopped her and Nick from getting married the summer between her junior and senior year of high school, Nick had disappeared that very night. She'd waited for months, hoping for a phone call, a letter—anything that would explain why he'd abandoned her. But there had been no word from him at all and she'd finally come to the conclusion that just as her father had said, Nick Daniels was trouble with a great big capital *T*. He hadn't even had the common courtesy or the courage to face her and tell her it was over between them.

But now he was back. And worse yet, he was her boss. How could fate be so cruel?

Seeing him again had been more than a little disturbing. But when he'd announced that he owned the Sugar Creek Cattle Company, the situation had become downright impossible.

She'd hoped when she questioned Mr. Freemont he would tell her that it was all a lie and that she had corporate's blessing in having Nick thrown off the property. But without elaborating on the details, Luther Freemont had verified that Nick Daniels did indeed own the Sugar Creek and that, in accordance with her contract, she was locked into working for the cattle company for the next four years, no matter who the owner was.

Parking her truck at the side of the big, white two-story Victorian house, she swallowed around the lump clogging her throat. She hadn't dared tell her father about the latest development. He wasn't well and hearing about Nick's return would only upset him and possibly cause more problems. And until she figured out what she could do about the situation there was no reason to worry him unnecessarily. Besides, she was doing enough stressing for the both of them.

As she grabbed the manila folder on the seat beside her and got out of the truck, she prayed for a miracle. She didn't really expect one, but at this point, divine intervention seemed to be her only hope of escaping the current mess she found herself in.

When she climbed the steps of the wide wrap-around porch and knocked on the door frame, instead of Nick, a heavy-set woman of about sixty opened the screen. "You must be Cheyenne Holbrook." She stepped back for Cheyenne to enter the foyer. "I'm Greta Foster. My husband, Carl, and I have been the caretakers here at the Sugar Creek for several years, but I don't believe we've had the pleasure of meeting."

Cheyenne wasn't surprised that they hadn't met. Before Nick left, her father had forbidden her to go anywhere near the place. And after she'd become the ranch foreman a little over six years ago, she hadn't ventured this far onto the Daniels property because it only reminded her of the shattered dream she'd had when she was sixteen.

She was supposed to have been Nick's wife and lived here with him and his mother in this big, wonderful house. While he ran the ranch, she was going to teach school and together they were going to raise a houseful of children and live happily ever after.

Removing her red ball cap, she shook her head to dispel the last traces of her troubling thoughts. "I've talked to Carl on the phone several times to let him know some of the men I supervise would be working close by, but I've never actually been here."

"Well, now that you have, you'll have to drop by more often." Greta's smile was friendly as she motioned toward a closed door across from the great room. "Nick's waiting for you in his office. Would you like something to eat or drink? I just took an apple pie out of the oven and made a fresh pot of coffee."

"No, thank you." Cheyenne smiled and raised her hand to knock on the office door. "I'm hoping this meeting won't take long." At Greta's surprised expression, Cheyenne hastily added, "I need to make a trip to the feed store for some supplies before Harry closes for lunch."

Apparently satisfied with her explanation, Greta nodded. "If you change your mind, I'll be in the kitchen."

As the woman moved down the hall toward the back of the house, Cheyenne took a moment to settle her jangled nerves. The last thing she wanted to do was go through with this meeting, but the choice had been taken out of her hands.

Before she could change her mind and run as far away as her old Ford truck could take her, she knocked, then opened the door. "Nick?"

He was sitting at a large oak desk, talking on the phone. "I'm glad to hear that you and Alyssa had a good time on your honeymoon in the Bahamas." Nodding for Cheyenne to come in and sit in the chair in front of his desk, Nick laughed at something the person on the other end of the line said. "Let me know when you hear more from Hunter about his E.M.T. courses. Talk to you later, Caleb."

When Nick hung up the phone and turned his attention on her, his easy expression faded. "I take it you spoke with Luther Freemont?"

Unable to relax, she sat on the edge of the leather armchair and pushed the folder across his desk. "Mr. Freemont told me that you were the owner of the Sugar Creek now and that I should discuss the terms of my contract with you."

His expression unreadable, he stared at her for several tense seconds before he picked up the file and flipped it open.

Cheyenne's cheeks grew increasingly warmer the longer he scanned the contents of the file. When she'd signed the contract to work for the cattle company, Mr. Freemont had assured her that the terms of their agreement would be handled with complete discretion and only a handful of people would know the real reason she'd signed away ten years of her life.

When Nick finally looked at her, his questioning expression had her wishing the floor would open up and swallow her. "Would you like to explain all this, Cheyenne?"

Humiliated beyond belief, she bit her lower lip to keep it from trembling. When she felt in control enough to get the words out, she proudly raised her head to meet his gaze head on.

"I think it's pretty self-explanatory." She took a deep breath. "Not only do you own the Sugar Creek, you own my father's ranch, as well."

Two

Nick couldn't have been more shocked if he'd been zapped by a juiced-up cattle prod. How ironic that the eighteen-year-old boy Judge Bertram Holbrook had tried his best to ruin all those years ago had not only returned to reclaim his ranch, he owned the good judge's ranch as well. If what the man had tried to do to him hadn't been so low and vindictive, Nick might have laughed out loud. But one look at Cheyenne's pretty face told him there was more behind the story than met the eye.

"All this contract tells me is that I own the Flying H and you have four more years left on a ten-year work agreement." Shoving the folder aside, he sat back in the leather desk chair. "Why don't you fill me in on the details?"

He could tell that was the last thing she wanted to do. But when she raised her eyes to meet his, there was a defiant pride in their aqua depths that he couldn't help but admire.

"Daddy had a stroke six years ago. He's been partially paralyzed on his left side and in a wheelchair ever since."

"I'm sorry to hear that, Cheyenne."

Nick knew how much she loved her father and how hard that had to have been for her. And no matter how much he despised the man, Nick didn't like to hear of anyone's suffering.

She glanced down at her hands. "When I dropped out of school to come home to care for him—"

"You had to quit school?" She'd always wanted to become a teacher and he hated that she'd had to give that up.

"I only had a couple of semesters left, but Daddy needed me more than I needed to finish school." She shrugged, but he could tell it still bothered her. "There wasn't any money for my last year at the university anyway."

Nick frowned. Bertram Holbrook had always been one of the wealthiest, most powerful men in the

county. Or at least, that's what he'd always led everyone to believe.

"Surely—"

"No." Obviously embarrassed, she suddenly rose
to her feet and walked over to the window between
the floor-to-ceiling bookshelves. "Do I have to spell
it out for you? We're broke. The only thing keeping
us from being homeless is that contract."

He didn't know what to say. As far as the judge
was concerned, Nick couldn't have cared less. But
Cheyenne didn't deserve the burden of having to pay
for the sins of her unscrupulous father or be forced
to give up her dreams.

"What happened?" he asked, when he finally
found his voice.

Her shoulders sagged as if the weight of the
world rested on them a moment before she finally
turned to face him. "Daddy had made some ill-
advised investments and when the stock market took
a nosedive, he was too incapacitated from the stroke
to sell before he lost most of his portfolio."

"He had a lot of Web site stocks?" Nick guessed,
remembering the crash of the Internet stocks several
years back.

"What was left wouldn't even cover our utility
bills for a month," she said, nodding. "Then, when

the doctors told us he couldn't work any longer, things went from bad to worse."

"What about insurance and a pension? He should have had the same paid benefits that other county and state officials have."

Something didn't ring true about the whole situation. Either the judge had been an extremely poor planner or his thirst for money and power had finally backfired on him. Nick suspected it was the latter that had finally brought the man down.

She walked back over and sank into the chair. "After Daddy had the stroke and couldn't work, there wasn't enough money to keep up the premiums on the insurance and he'd withdrawn everything in his pension fund to invest in the stocks."

Nick would have thought the judge had more sense than to deplete every resource he had. But then, greed could do that. And if there was ever a more greedy, power-mad human being than Bertram Holbrook, Nick had never met him.

"You didn't know any of this?"

"No." She rubbed her forehead with a trembling hand. "Daddy never discussed finances with me. He always told me that I'd never have to worry about those things."

Nick would bet every dime he had that finances weren't the only things the man had kept her in the dark about. "I'm sure it all came as quite a shock when you found out."

She nodded. "I had no idea what we were going to do. Fortunately Emerald, Inc. contacted me about buying the Flying H right after I came to the conclusion there was no alternative but for us to file for bankruptcy." Her cheeks colored a deep rose. "Then, when it became clear there wasn't enough money from the sale of the ranch to pay off Daddy's medical and rehabilitation bills, Mr. Freemont told me the corporation would pay off the rest of our creditors, allow us to stay in our home and pay me a modest salary if I signed a ten-year contract to be the ranch foreman of the newly formed Sugar Creek Cattle Company. At the end of that time, our debts will be considered paid in full and I'll be free to renegotiate my contract or move on."

If Nick had thought things were strange before, they'd just taken a turn toward bizarre. But the more he thought about it, the more it sounded like Emerald had learned of the Holbrook's money problems and, in the bargain, seized the opportunity to mete out a bit of revenge for the judge's treatment of him and his mother all those years ago.

Unfortunately it wasn't Bertram Holbrook who was having to pay the price for Emerald's retaliatory actions. Cheyenne was the one who'd practically sold herself into servitude to bail the old man out of his financial woes. And it didn't sit well with Nick one damned bit that his indominable grandmother had obviously been taking advantage of Cheyenne.

"Do you mind if I keep this for a couple of days to look over?" he asked, picking up the contract. If there was a way to get them both out of this mess, he intended to find it. "I need to figure out if you owe me or Emerald, Inc."

She shrugged one slender shoulder as she rose to her feet. "You might as well, since it appears that I work for you now, instead of Emerald, Inc."

"Where are you going?"

From the look on her face, she couldn't wait to end their meeting. "Unless you have something more you want to discuss, I've got work to do."

He did, but first he wanted to talk to Emerald. "I'll go over this and see what the exact wording is, then we'll discuss it tomorrow afternoon while we inspect the herds."

"Can't you do that on your own?" She sounded close to going into a panic at the thought of spending time with him.

Nick smiled. "I could, but it's standard practice for the foreman to show the new owner around. Besides, I'm sure I'll have a few questions about the way you've been running the operation."

Clearly unhappy, she hesitated a moment before she nodded. "Fine." Walking to the door, she turned back. "I'll be here tomorrow after lunch. Be ready."

"I'll have the horses saddled."

"The truck would be faster."

"I'd rather ride."

She glared at him for several long seconds before she finally nodded. "All right…boss." Then, opening the door, she walked out into the hall and slammed it shut behind her.

Once he was alone, Nick inhaled deeply. He hadn't drawn a decent breath since Cheyenne had walked into the room. He wouldn't have believed it was possible, but she was even prettier today than she'd been yesterday. Her turquoise T-shirt had brought out the blue-green of her eyes and the sun shining through the window behind her when she'd turned to face him had accentuated the golden highlights in her long brown hair.

His temperature soared at the mental image and shaking his head at his own foolishness, he did his best to ignore the tightening in his groin. But then, it had always been that way with Cheyenne. From the first moment he saw her at the homecoming dance his senior year, he hadn't been able to think of anything but making her his wife and living out the rest of his days trying to prove himself worthy of her.

Thinking back on that summer after his high school graduation, he still couldn't get over how naive they'd been. He and Cheyenne had gone steady throughout his senior year, even though her father had forbidden her to have anything to do with Nick. Neither of them had understood the judge's intense dislike of Nick, but they'd managed to sneak around to see each other at school functions and met in town every Saturday afternoon to hug and kiss their way through a double-feature matinee at the movie theater. And despite Bertram Holbrook's concentrated efforts to keep them from seeing each other, by the end of the summer they'd fallen in love and were desperate to be together.

Nick couldn't remember which one of them had hatched up the plan to run away and get married. Truth to tell, it really didn't matter. It was what they'd both wanted and they'd heard that for a couple of hundred bucks the clerk over in the next county would issue a marriage license to anyone, whether they were of legal age or not. So he'd worked at the feed store on weekends and saved every dime he could until he had enough to make Cheyenne his bride.

Then, one hot night in late August, he'd picked her up at the house of one of her friends and they'd driven across the county line to get married. But just before they were pronounced husband and wife, the judge and his cohort, Sheriff Turner, had shown up to stop the ceremony.

Nick rubbed the tension gathering at the back of his neck. Until yesterday afternoon, his last remembrance of Cheyenne had been watching her sob uncontrollably as her father led her away from the little church to his car.

But things had a way of working out for the best. Marrying his high school sweetheart had been the lofty illusion of an eighteen-year-old boy with more hormones than good sense. He was a grown man now and no matter how alluring he found Cheyenne, there was no danger of falling under her spell a second time.

Besides, after discovering that his father was an irresponsible player who had thought nothing of walking out on not one, but three women he'd impregnated, who was to say that Nick hadn't inherited the same "love 'em and leave 'em" gene? After all, he was the one who'd lost interest in every relationship he'd had since leaving Wyoming.

Picking up the contract, he scanned the contents of the document a little closer. There had to be a clause concerning termination of the agreement—a way to free them from having to work together.

His frown turned to a deep scowl when he found it. In the event that Cheyenne quit or her position as foreman was terminated for any reason, the balance of the money immediately became due and payable to Emerald, Inc. No exceptions.

He should have known Emerald would cover all the bases. She hadn't gained the reputation of being an invincible force in the boardroom or become one of the richest, most successful businesswomen in America by accident.

As he dialed his grandmother's private number, he took a deep breath to control his anger. Although he no longer had feelings for Cheyenne, he didn't like the idea of Emerald taking advantage of her or circumstances that were beyond her control.

Instead of Emerald, Luther Freemont answered. "I'm sorry, Mr. Daniels. Your grandmother is unavailable at the moment. May I take a message?"

Nick could tell the man had him on the speakerphone and knew the old gal was probably sitting right there at the desk listening to every word he said while her assistant ran interference for her. "Maybe you can help me, Luther. I have a few questions about Cheyenne Holbrook's employment with the Sugar Creek Cattle Company."

There was a long pause before the man spoke. "What would that be, sir?"

"I'd like some more information on Ms. Holbrook's salary, the balance on what she owes Emerald, Inc. and if she's my employee or Emerald's."

Another long pause signaled that the man was most likely looking to Emerald for direction. "I'm not at liberty to say, sir. I'm afraid you'll have to discuss that with Mrs. Larson."

Irritated with the entire situation, Nick muttered a pithy curse. "Tell Emerald to give me a call as soon as possible."

"I'll be sure to do that. Is there anything else I can help you with, sir?"

Nick couldn't resist teasing Emerald's stiff and formal personal assistant. "As a matter of fact, there is, Luther."

"Yes, sir?"

"You sound like a robot. Loosen up and stop being such a tightass."

"I'll take that under advisement, sir," the man said with a hint of laughter in his voice.

Nick grinned when he heard the definitive sound of a woman laughing in the background a moment before the connection ended.

"Daddy, I have to go up to the summer pastures to check the herds this afternoon," Cheyenne said as she put their lunch plates in the dishwasher. "Will you be all right until I get back?"

Her father nodded as he backed his wheelchair away from the table. "I'll be fine, princess. Gordon called this morning to tell me he's going to stop by for a while." He chuckled. "I'm sure he's got some hot piece of gossip he'd like to share."

Cheyenne smiled wanly. She'd never cared for Sheriff Turner, but he and her father had been friends for over twenty years and her father always looked forward to his visits.

She kissed her father's cheek. "There's some lemonade in the refrigerator and peanut butter cookies in the cookie jar if you two get hungry."

Smiling, he patted her arm. "What would I do without you, princess?"

"I'm sure you'd do just fine, but that's something you won't ever have to worry about." Checking her watch, she gave him a quick hug, then grabbed her truck keys from the counter. "You and Sheriff Turner stay out of trouble."

Her father laughed. "Now what could a county sheriff and a crippled old judge possibly do to get themselves in hot water?"

"Let me think." Tapping her index finger on her chin, she acted as if she had to give it a lot of consideration. "I'm sure you'll turn down the extra cigar that Sheriff Turner just happens to bring with him?"

"Of course I'll turn it down. Just like I always do." Her father's eyes twinkled mischievously. "I wouldn't think to do anything else, princess."

They both knew he was telling a fib. The sheriff always tried to time his visits to coincide with her working on another part of the ranch in order for her father to smoke a cigar—something his doctors had advised him to cut out. But he had very few pleasures left in life and she decided the occasional cigar he enjoyed once or twice a month while he visited with his best friend wasn't going to do that much harm.

Smiling, she opened the door to leave. "Just remember, if the sheriff wants to have a cigar there's no smoking in the house. You'll both have to go out onto the back porch."

Her father waved for her to leave. "You just be careful out there in the pastures. You might run across a wolf, or worse."

Cheyenne's stomach twisted into a tight knot. She wouldn't encounter a wolf somewhere along the way, she'd be riding right along beside one.

Nodding, she ducked out the door before he had a chance to see the guilt she knew had to be written all over her face. It had been three days since she'd run across Nick repairing that section of fence and she still hadn't found the courage to tell her father about him being back in the area or that he owned the very house they lived in.

For one thing, she wasn't sure how her father would react. He'd already had one stroke. She certainly didn't want to run the risk of him having another when he learned that she was working for Nick. And for another, she didn't want or need to listen to him tell her how disreputable Nick was or that she'd do well to steer clear of him. She knew firsthand how unreliable Nick was.

Cheyenne sighed heavily as she climbed into her truck and drove the five miles to the Sugar Creek ranch house. She really didn't have a lot of choice in the matter. Even if they figured out who held the promissory note—Emerald, Inc. or Nick—heaven only knew she didn't have the money to repay it in order to get out of the work agreement.

Ten minutes later, when she pulled into the ranch yard and got out of the truck, the first thing she noticed was the bay and sorrel geldings standing saddled and tied to the corral fence. They were waiting for her to take Nick to see the cattle company herds— his herds. But he was nowhere in sight. And that suited her just fine. The less time she had to spend with him the better off she'd be.

Walking over to the horses, she patted the sorrel gelding's neck. She'd been more humiliated than she'd ever been in her life during their meeting yesterday when she'd had to tell him that she and her father were practically destitute. But that hadn't stopped her from noticing that the boy she'd once loved with all her heart had grown into a devastatingly handsome man or that whenever he turned his deep blue eyes her way, her chest tightened with an ache she'd thought she'd long ago gotten over.

"You're late."

Her stomach did a little flip at the sound of Nick's deep baritone and, turning around, she found him standing with one shoulder propped against the edge of the barn door, his arms crossed over his wide chest. She swallowed hard and tried not to notice how his chambray shirt emphasized the width of his shoulders or how his worn jeans hugged his muscular thighs and rode low on his narrow hips. As he pushed away from the barn and walked toward her, her pulse sped up and she felt as if she couldn't breathe.

"I had things to do," she said, hating the breathless tone of her own voice. "Besides, this shouldn't take long. Both herds are pastured within a few miles' ride of each other."

He nodded as he untied the two horses, then handed her the sorrel's reins. "I need to be back before supper."

"We'll be back well before then," she said, mounting the gelding.

"Good. I have plans."

Cheyenne couldn't believe the twinge of disappointment coursing through her. She couldn't care less if he had a date. She really couldn't. As long as he left her alone, he could date and bed the county's entire female population and it wouldn't bother her one bit.

"If you'd like to postpone checking the herds, it won't bother me. I have other things I need to be doing anyway."

He effortlessly swung up onto the bay and rode up beside her. "No, I want to see what we've got so that when I go to the auction tomorrow night, I can compare what we have to what's being sold. Then I'll have a fair idea of how much I can get when I sell our cattle."

"You're selling out?"

Panic sent a cold chill snaking up her spine and caused her stomach to twist into a painful knot. If he sold everything, how was she supposed to pay off the remainder of her debt?

"Don't worry, you'll still have a job," he said as if he'd read her mind. "I'm starting a new breeding program that will make the Sugar Creek a major force to contend with in the beef industry. And I can't do that with the cattle we have now."

"You're not going to start raising some obscure breed that no one has ever heard of, are you?"

"Not hardly." Laughing, he shook his head as they

nudged the horses into a slow walk. "The Sugar Creek has always raised Black Angus and we always will. The same as the Flying H. But they're going to be free-range cattle. No more supplements, growth hormones or commercial cattle feed. We're starting an all-natural operation."

Relieved to hear that she wouldn't have to worry about finding a way to pay back money she didn't have—at least for now—she nodded. "Free-range stock of all kinds are becoming very popular."

"It's getting bigger by the day and we're missing out on a fast-growing market." When he turned his head to look at her, he adjusted the wide brim of his black Resistol so that their gazes met. "The way I figure it, between the two ranches there's a little over a hundred and fifty thousand acres of prime grazing land and plenty of good grass to cut for hay to feed the cattle in the winter months."

He definitely had her interest. It could take several years for an operation like that to reach its peak. Maybe if he was busy planning how many acres he'd use for graze, how many for hay and where and how to market the beef, she'd be free to do her job and get through the next four years of her contract without having a lot of contact with him.

"When are you going to start selling off the herds and bringing in the new stock?"

"Within the next couple of weeks. I'm going to talk to the auction house tomorrow night about selling off the cattle in lots of ten to fifteen. I think I'll get more out of them that way."

She frowned. With the cold Wyoming winter just around the corner, it seemed like a bad time to be bringing in a new herd. "When will the new stock arrive?"

"Next spring."

Glancing over at him as they rode across the pasture behind his house, she couldn't help but wonder where she fit into the equation. With no stock to feed or any need to chop ice for the cattle to get water from the ponds and streams this winter there really wasn't going to be any work for her to supervise.

When they reached a gate at the back of the pasture, she started to dismount, but Nick was quicker and jumped down from the bay to open it. "I'm betting you're wondering what you'll be doing with your time this winter."

She led the bay as she rode the sorrel through the opening into the next field. "Well, now that you mention it, it did cross my mind."

He chuckled. "Don't worry. There'll be more than enough work for both of us." Taking the bay's reins, he swung back up into the saddle. "After the herds are sold, we'll be busy planning how many acres per head of cattle we'll need, how we intend to rotate them and how many acres of hay we'll need to cut in the summer to get them through the winter."

Her heart skipped a beat. "We? Why can't you do that yourself?"

He stared off across the Sugar Creek Valley at the Laramie Mountains in the distance. "I'm changing your job description. From now on, you'll be working in the office and I'll be out supervising the men and managing the daily operation."

"Excuse me?" She reined in the gelding at the edge of the creek the ranch had been named for. "What office are you talking about?"

Stopping the bay, he shrugged. "My office at the Sugar Creek."

Cheyenne felt a chill travel from the top of her head to the soles of her feet. How on earth was she going to keep her distance from him if she had to work in his office? In his home?

"You mean until the new cattle arrive in the spring?"

He shook his head. "From now on. I've missed being out in the fresh air and feeling like I've actually accomplished something when I go to bed so tired that I'm asleep before my head hits the pillow."

She couldn't help it, she laughed out loud as she urged the sorrel across the slow moving, shallow water of Sugar Creek. "Give me a break. You can't tell me you'd rather be out in weather so cold your breath freezes on your lips or so hot that you feel like your brains are baking inside your hat."

"I'm serious, Cheyenne." He rode up the bank on the other side of the creek. "I've been stuck being a desk jockey for the past eight years and I'm tired of it."

It wasn't any of her business nor did she care what he'd been doing for the past thirteen years, but curiosity got the better of her. "What kind of job did you have?"

"I developed software for a bank's online customers to pay bills and transfer funds from one account to another."

"You graduated from college." She couldn't keep from sounding wistful.

"Yep. I have a degree in software development and computer applications."

"And you gave up all that to come back here to shovel manure and cut yourself to ribbons stringing barbed wire fence? Are you nuts?"

He grinned. "Put that way, it doesn't sound real smart, does it?"

Laughing, Cheyenne shook her head. "I'll bet your mother is very proud of you for earning your degree, but fit to be tied that you won't be using it. She always wanted you to go to college." It suddenly occurred to her that she hadn't asked about his mother. "By the way, how is she doing?"

His smile faded and stopping his horse at the top of a rise, he gazed out over the herd of sleek black cattle grazing in the shallow valley below. "Mom died about a year after we moved to St. Louis. She never knew that I went to college, let alone graduated."

"Oh, Nick, I'm so sorry. I didn't know." She'd always liked Linda Daniels and hated to hear of the woman's passing. "Had she been ill?"

Cheyenne knew from experience how hard his mother's death had to have been for Nick. She'd lost her own mother when she was very young and had it not been for the love of her father, she wasn't sure she would have survived. But Nick hadn't had anyone to lean on. His mother had never married and it had always been just the two of them.

"Mom knew she didn't have long to live when we left here," he said quietly.

"Was that why you went to St. Louis? I think I remember you mentioning that your mother had a cousin there."

Nick turned to stare at Cheyenne. The sincerity in her blue-green eyes convinced him that she didn't have a clue why he'd run away in the middle of the night like a coyote with a backside full of buckshot. And that had him wondering just what the good judge had told her about his disappearance the night they were to have been married.

"That's where we went to live," he said, turning his attention back to the herd of cattle in the valley below. "But that wasn't the reason we left here."

He could tell from her intense stare that she was baffled by his answer, but she didn't pursue the issue further. Instead she reined her horse toward the path leading down into the meadow. But the gelding balked, then gingerly held his front hoof off the ground as if it might be injured.

"I think we have a problem," Nick said as they both dismounted to examine the sorrel's left front leg. Bending down, he gently examined the inside center of the animal's hoof. "The sole looks swollen."

"It's probably a stone bruise."

Straightening, he nodded. "That would be my guess. Looks like we'll have to ride double."

She shook her head as she patted the gelding's neck. "It's only a few miles. You go ahead and I'll walk him back."

"I don't think so, sweetheart." He took the reins from her. "There's no way in hell I'm going to ride back to the house and leave you out here alone with a lame horse."

"You can go faster without me." She took a step back. "You said yourself that you have a date tonight and I certainly don't want to be the cause of you being late."

Nick stared at her for several long seconds. Had there been a bit of sarcasm in her voice?

He knew he should let it go, but some part of him had to know. "Does it bother you that I might be seeing someone, Cheyenne?"

"Not at all." Her laughter was as hollow as the old bee tree out behind his barn. "I don't know why you'd wonder something like that. I gave up caring what you do a long time ago."

He knew she was lying and for reasons beyond his comprehension, he wanted her to admit the truth. "You never could lie worth a damn, sweetheart."

"I'm not lying."

"Yes, you are." He stepped forward and putting his arm around her waist, drew her to him. Lowering his voice, he whispered close to her ear. "You don't like caring, but you do."

"D-don't flatter yourself, Nick Daniels. What you do or who you do it with is none of my concern."

"Is that so?"

"Absolutely."

The breathless tone of her voice and the tremor he felt pass through her slender body belied her words and, unable to stop himself, Nick pushed the brim of her ball cap up out of the way and lowered his head. "Let's just settle the issue here and now."

Three

When Nick covered her mouth with his, Cheyenne's heart began to pound like she'd run a marathon and every cell in her body tingled to life. She tried to remain unaffected, tried to fight the heat filling every fiber of her being. She didn't want to feel anything for him but contempt.

This was the man who had broken her young heart all those years ago, the man who had left her behind without a word or even a backward glance. He'd proven what her father had said about him to be right on the money—there wasn't anything more to Nick Daniels than a handful of empty promises and a boatload of heartaches. But try as she might, she couldn't stop the honeyed warmth flowing through her veins or the overwhelming need to kiss him back.

At eighteen, Nick the boy had kissed her with the soft, innocent reverence of youthful love. But as his lips moved over hers now, then urged her to open for him, she found that Nick the man kissed her with a thoroughness that caused her head to spin and made every bone in her body feel as if it had been turned to rubber.

When he tightened his hold and she felt the hard contours of his body pressed to her much softer curves, her pulse throbbed and she gave up all pretense of resisting. His breathtaking exploration of her tender inner recesses stole her breath and wiped out all thought of the past, present or future. At the moment, all she wanted to do was savor the delicious sensations flowing from the top of her head all the way to her curled toes inside her scuffed boots.

With her hands trapped between them, she had to grasp his shirt in order to keep her balance. But the flexing of his rock-hard pectoral muscles beneath the fabric sent her pulse racing and caused her knees to give way completely. Moving his hands from her back to cup her bottom, he positioned his leg between hers to help support her.

Cheyenne's heart stopped, then took off like a

runaway train at the feel of his strong thigh wedged against the most feminine part of her. A flash of un-expected need, so strong it sent shivers up her spine, streaked through her and caused her to moan from the sheer pleasure of it.

The uncharacteristic sound shocked her back to reality and pushing against him, she shook her head. "No. Stop."

He immediately set her away from him, then step-ping back gave her a look that sent her temperature up at least ten degrees. "I guess we settled that, didn't we, sweetheart?"

His confident comment and knowing smile were as effective as a bucket of ice water and chased away all traces of desire. "I suppose we did." She took the sor-rel's reins and, leading the injured animal, started walk-ing back the way they'd come. "I'm sorry to disappoint you, Nick, but you're going to have to face facts. That spark we used to have between us is long gone."

Before she'd gone two steps, his hand on her arm stopped her. "Is that why you were clinging to me? Or why you brought up my going out on a date in the first place?"

Cheyenne stared at his large hand wrapped around her upper arm a moment before she pulled away from his grasp. "I merely pointed out that you'll be late if you insist that we ride back to the house together." She gave him a smile that she hoped with all her heart set his teeth on edge. "You're the one who seems to think it should matter. Not me."

"Whatever you say, Cheyenne." Grinning, he shook his head as he took the sorrel's reins from her and dallied them to the bay's saddle horn. "Come on. We're wasting time."

She wasn't looking forward to walking three miles in boots, but it was preferable to riding double with him. Especially after that kiss.

"You go on. I'll walk."

"This isn't negotiable."

Mounting the bay, Nick held his hand out to help Cheyenne up onto the horse. She didn't look any happier about the situation than he was, but, grasping his arm, she allowed him to pull her up to sit behind him on the gelding's broad back.

They rode in silence for some time and it wasn't lost on him that she held on to the back of the saddle instead of wrapping her arms around his waist. And that suited him just fine. The less physical contact they had, the better.

What the hell had he been thinking when he'd taken her in his arms, anyway? Why had it been so imperative that he make her admit it bothered her to think of him with another woman?

He'd acted like some kind of macho jerk out to

prove a point. And the only thing he'd succeeded in doing was proving to himself that he was more like his father than he wanted to admit.

From everything Nick had heard about Owen Larson, he'd been the kind of man who used the steamroller approach with women—overpowering them with his charm, seducing them in order to prove to himself that he could. And although Nick hadn't kissed Cheyenne with seduction in mind or because he wanted to prove his virility, he had wanted to overwhelm her and make her admit that she still cared for him.

As they crossed Sugar Creek and started up the bank on the other side, he felt as if he'd been struck by a bolt of lightning when Cheyenne had to put her arms around him for a more secure hold. The warmth of her body and the feel of her breasts pressed to his back did strange things to his insides and had him struggling to draw his next breath.

He'd gotten over her years ago and he had absolutely no interest in rekindling anything they'd once shared. But that didn't stop his body from responding to her in a way that made sitting astride a horse damned uncomfortable, if not dangerous.

Deciding he needed to put a little space between them or risk emasculating himself, he pulled his horse to a stop. "We'll let the sorrel rest a bit before we go on."

"I think that's a good idea," she said, sliding from the back of the bay.

After he let the horses get a drink, Nick ground-tied them to graze, then joined Cheyenne, sitting under the shade of a large cottonwood tree. Wanting to ease the tension between them, he searched for a neutral topic.

"Catch me up on all that's happened around here since I've been gone."

"There hasn't been much." She shrugged as she plucked a blade of grass to twirl it between her slender fingers. "Your friend, Tom Little Bear, is making a career in the Marines. He married a North Carolina girl while he was stationed at Camp Lejeune and the last I heard, they had four children and another one on the way."

Nick laughed. "That sounds like Bear. He always said he wanted a big family."

Cheyenne smiled. "His sister, Marleen, has eight children."

"What about your friends?" he asked casually. "Did Sally Hanley finally convince Doug Carson to take a trip down the aisle?"

"Yes, but they couldn't make it work. They divorced after three years and Sally ended up marrying Gerald Reynolds. They run the Bucket of Suds Bar and Grill in Elk Bluff."

They sat in silence for some time as Nick as-
similated all the changes that had taken place in the
thirteen years he'd been gone. But as he sat there pon-
dering everything Cheyenne had told him about their
friends, he couldn't help but wonder if she'd found
someone special.

The thought caused a burning in his gut and had
him wondering if he'd lost his mind. It was none of
his business who she'd seen after he left. He'd for-
feited that right a long time ago.

Standing up, he offered his hand to help her to her
feet. "Are you ready to go?"

When she nodded and took his hand a charge of
electricity streaked up his arm, then spread throughout his chest. She must have felt it too because once
she stood up she dropped his hand so fast he was surprised she didn't end up hurting her wrist.

"You're not the only one who needs to get home,"
she said, checking her watch.

Grinning, he teased, "Got a hot date?"

She gave him a smile that sent his blood pressure
sky high. "As a matter of fact, I do."

He instantly stopped grinning and the burning in
his gut that he'd experienced earlier at the thought of
her with another man returned with a vengeance.
"Then we'd better get going." He caught the horses
and mounting the bay, he pulled her up behind him.

"When you see loverboy tonight, tell him that you won't be available tomorrow evening."

"Why?"

"You'll be working."

Her glare could have melted metal. "And just what will I be doing?"

Traditionally, ranchers gave their hired help Saturday night off. But for reasons he wouldn't even allow himself to consider, he didn't want Cheyenne available to anyone but him.

"I've decided to take you to the stock auction with me."

As Nick watched the Cardinals shut out the Diamondbacks, he struggled with his insistance that Cheyenne accompany him to the stock auction tomorrow night. He hadn't originally intended to take her along. So what the hell had gotten into him?

He'd found it rather humorous when she'd mistakenly thought his plans for the evening included a woman. But her admission that she had a date tonight had tied him up in such a knot that it had damned near knocked him to his knees. And for the life of him, he couldn't figure out why.

What they'd once had together was past history and it would be completely unreasonable for him to expect her not to have moved on with her life. He had. And although he wasn't overly proud of the fact that he hadn't been able to sustain a relationship for longer than a few months without losing interest, it wasn't like he hadn't had his share of women in the years since they'd parted ways.

But whether it was rational or not, just the thought of Cheyenne in the arms of another man sent a searing pain straight to the pit of his belly and had him ready to punch something or somebody.

Taking a swig of beer from the longneck bottle in his hand, he shook his head as he blindly stared at the ball game. He had a feeling he knew exactly what his problem was. When he and Cheyenne had been kids sneaking around behind her father's back to be together, he'd never crossed the line with her, never taken her virginity and truly made her his. Not that he hadn't wanted to or that she wouldn't have been willing. But Nick had been determined not to be anything like the man who'd gotten his mother pregnant, then left her high and dry to face the consequences. And that meant not making love to Cheyenne until he'd done the right thing and made her his wife.

He took a deep breath. He didn't expect her to still be a virgin at the age of twenty-nine, but the thought that some other man had touched her and taken her innocence was enough to turn him wrong side out. That was supposed to have been his claim, his right as her husband. But that was no longer an issue after all this time.

Shaking his head, he closed his eyes and leaned his head back against the chair. Thirteen years ago, his obsession with her and her father's unexplained hatred of him damn near cost him a prison sentence and he wasn't about to jeopardize the chance Emerald had given him to reclaim what was rightfully his. But the truth of the matter was, he still wanted Cheyenne physically. He wasn't happy about wanting her. But he did. It was just that simple.

As he questioned his sanity, a thought suddenly occurred to him. He was no longer that green as grass kid he'd been back then and Cheyenne was no longer jailbait. And although he had no intention of becoming emotionally involved with her or any other woman, he couldn't think of one good reason why they couldn't enjoy a satisfying physical relationship.

He knew for certain she was as attracted to him as he was to her. And as long as they kept it all in perspective and their emotions in check, there shouldn't be a problem.

Now, the uppermost question on his mind was how to go about convincing Cheyenne that it was the best way for both of them to get each other out of their systems once and for all.

* * *

Cheyenne kept her head lowered as she preceded Nick through the crowded auction barn and up the bleachers to find a couple of empty seats. She wasn't the least bit happy about being seen out in public with him. Nearly all of the ranchers and ranch foremen attending the sale knew her and her father and she was positive that several of them remembered Nick. And although he'd changed a lot in thirteen years, she had no doubt that someone would recognize him.

Normally that wouldn't be a big deal. She was Nick's employee and there was absolutely nothing going on between them. But she'd yet to tell her father that Nick was back in the area, let alone that he was the new owner of the Sugar Creek. What if one of her father's acquaintances mentioned that they'd seen her at the auction with Nick before she found a way to break the news of his return?

Slumping into one of the chairs, she pulled the bill of her ball cap a little lower and prayed that the first lot of cattle would be herded into the arena soon. Once the auctioneer started the bidding, everyone's attention would be focused on the action in the ring and off the matter of who was in attendance.

"You're awfully quiet," Nick said as he settled into the seat beside her.

"I'm just waiting for the sale to start." She glanced

around to see if anyone noticed them. Breathing a little easier when she found that no one seemed interested, she asked, "Did you talk to the manager? Is he agreeable to auctioning off lots of ten to fifteen head of cattle at a time?"

Nick nodded as he looked over the sale bill. "I called earlier today and he said he'd be more than happy to accommodate my request."

She frowned. "If you've already made the arrangements, then why are we here?"

"Prices. I want to see what the going rate is so that I can calculate what I think we'll get for the herds."

"You could have done that yourself."

"I wanted company," he said, shrugging.

Glaring at him, she folded her arms beneath her breasts and without thinking, muttered, "You could have asked your date from last night to accompany you. I'm sure she would have been a lot happier to be here than I am."

Nick's slow smile made her warm all over, but just as he opened his mouth to comment on her ill-chosen words, the auctioneer welcomed everyone to the night's event and instructed the gate man to let the first animals up for bidding into the arena. It appeared that she'd been saved from having to explain herself, at least for the time being.

Over the next few hours, she began to relax a bit as she watched a procession of cattle, horses and sheep herded into the arena—some individually, some in lots. Surely by the end of the auction Nick would forget that she'd mentioned his date again.

What she couldn't understand was why she kept bringing it up. She didn't care that he was seeing another woman. She really didn't. And maybe if she kept telling herself enough times, she might even start to believe it.

But when the gavel came down for the final time and Nick took her hand to keep them from being separated in the crowd departing the auction barn, his smile told her that he not only hadn't forgotten her slip of the tongue, but he had every intention of commenting on it.

"Would you like to know what my plans were last night, Cheyenne?" he asked as they walked the short distance to his truck.

"No." She didn't particularly want to hear the details, even if she didn't care that he was seeing someone.

"Are you sure?"

"Yes." Why was he being so persistent?

"I'll tell you about my evening, if you'll tell me about yours."

His eyes lit with mischief and she could tell he

wasn't going to let the matter drop. "Oh, good heavens! Tell me and get it over with."

Opening the passenger door to his truck, he smiled. "Ladies first."

Thinking quickly, she smiled. "I took Sebastian MacDougal to bed with me and spent the entire evening with him."

Nick's expression turned dark. "Who the hell is this Sebastian character?"

"Just someone I know," she said, shrugging as she climbed into the truck.

"Is he from around here?"

"Not that it's any of your concern, but no. He's not from around here." Smiling, she buckled her shoulder harness. "He's from the United Kingdom."

She almost laughed out loud at the deep scowl on Nick's handsome face. If only her evening had been as exciting as what she'd just described. But she wasn't about to admit that the man in question was the hero in a suspense novel she'd been reading.

"What about your evening?" she asked when he walked around the front of the truck and slid in behind the steering wheel. "I've told you about mine. Now it's your turn."

"Mine wasn't anywhere near as wild as yours." He gave her a look that made her warm all over as he started the truck's engine. "I stayed home and watched the Cardinals kick the Diamondbacks' butts, then I went to bed. Alone."

"What happened?" she asked before she could stop herself. "Was your date canceled?"

"No. I did exactly what I intended to do. I watched the ball game."

"But you said—"

He shook his head as he put the truck in gear and steered it from the parking lot. "I told you I had plans and that I wanted to get back home before supper. You were the one who insisted that I had a date."

His evening hadn't included a woman? No wonder he'd been amused when he asked her if she was bothered by the thought of him seeing someone. Her reaction had confirmed that it did.

"Why didn't you correct me?" She wasn't about to take all the blame for the misunderstanding. After all, he hadn't made the slightest attempt to set the record straight.

He smiled. "I had my reasons."

Not wanting to listen to him tell her how transparent she'd been, she decided it would be in her best interest to change the subject. "Did you find out who I owe in the event I find myself without a job at the Sugar Creek?"

"I'm still waiting on a call from Emerald, Inc. for clarification, but the best I can decipher from your contract, you're in the clear as long as you continue to work for me." He shook his head. "If you're worried about being out of a job—don't. I have no plans to replace you or anyone else."

On the one hand, it was a relief to know she wouldn't have to come up with the thousands of dollars it would take to pay off the debt. But on the other hand, it appeared there was no way out of working for Nick for the next several years.

"It doesn't make sense to me how I can work for you and the Sugar Creek Cattle Company and still owe Emerald Inc. I would have thought that when you bought the cattle company, you'd have also gained control of my contract." She stared out the windshield at the brilliant display of stars dotting the midnight sky. "Is it just me, or is there something about this whole deal that doesn't add up?"

Unwilling to admit that the Sugar Creek had been given to him or that the mighty Emerald Larson was his newfound grandmother, Nick made no comment. Hell, he hadn't gotten used to the idea himself. Besides, he needed to talk to Emerald before he discussed things with Cheyenne.

On the surface, it did look like she and her father should owe him the balance of the loan. But Nick had a feeling that Emerald fully intended to retain control of Cheyenne's contract until it was completely paid off. What he couldn't figure out was why. And until he talked to his domineering grandmother, it would be best to keep quiet.

When he steered the truck into the yard and parked beside the house, he started to get out and open the passenger door, but Cheyenne beat him to it. She was already halfway to her truck when he managed to stop her.

"Would you like to come in for a while?"

"I don't think that would be a good idea," she said, shaking her head.

Without thinking, Nick reached out and loosely circled her waist with his arms. "What's the matter? Are you afraid Sebastian will find out?"

She placed her hands flat on his chest, but instead of shoving him away, her fingers seemed to caress his chest muscles through the fabric of his shirt. "M-maybe."

"How serious are you about this Sebastian character?" he asked, wondering how far she'd take the ruse.

"Why do you care?" She sounded slightly winded.

"I don't." Pushing the wide brim of his Resistol back, he lowered his head to nuzzle the satiny skin along the column of her neck. "When are you going to admit that Sebastian is the lead character in Baxter Armstrong's latest mystery novel?"

To his immense satisfaction, she shivered against

him. "Wh-what makes you think that Sebastian's fictional?"

He laughed. "I read the book a couple of weeks ago."

"Then why—"

Kissing the frown from her forehead, he smiled. "I wanted to see just how far you'd go with your little story."

She shook her head. "It wasn't a story. I told the truth. I took the book to bed with me and woke up this morning with it on the mattress beside me. I can't help that you assumed I was having a wildly erotic night with someone."

Nick knew that he should let well enough alone and drop the matter. Instead he found himself pulling her closer. For reasons he'd rather not dwell on, he wanted to wipe out the memory of the men in her past, to make her forget anyone but him.

"This is insane, Nick." He felt a slight tremor pass through her at the contact of her body pressed closely to his. "What we had between us is ancient history."

"You're right, sweetheart." Tightening his arms around her, he lowered his head to brush her mouth with his. "I'm not concerned with the past. It's the present that I want to explore."

As his mouth settled over hers, he could tell she was trying to remain impassive, trying to deny the myriad the sensations coursing between them. But when he coaxed her to open for him, she readily complied and melted against him.

Encouraged by her response, Nick savored the taste of her and the feel of her soft body pressed to his. Her breasts crushed to his chest, the nipples taut with longing scored his skin through the fabric of his shirt and caused a flash fire to race through every fiber of his being.

But when she wrapped her arms around his waist and shyly stroked his tongue with hers, the heat gathering in the pit of his belly tightened his groin with an intensity that robbed him of breath. He wanted her. And if the way she was clinging to him was any indication, she wanted him just as much.

Moving his hands from her back, then up along her sides, he slid them to the underside of her breasts. Her impatient whimper and the tightening of her arms around his waist when he paused assured him that she wanted his touch. Cupping the soft mounds through the layers of her clothing, he gently caressed and teased the tight tips until she moaned with pleasure.

The sound of her own passion seemed to startle her, and he knew from the sudden rigidity of her slender frame that the moment was over.

Nick eased away from the kiss, then stepping back, he smiled down at her. "Be here first thing

Monday morning. We need to start making decisions about dividing up the herds."

She blinked, then propping her fists on her shapely little hips, gave him a look that would have dropped a lesser man dead in his tracks. "I don't know what game you're playing here, Nick Daniels. But you can count me out."

If he'd ever seen a more beautiful woman, he couldn't remember when. Even with her ponytail threaded through the back of an old red ball cap and a frown marring her pretty features, she could easily win the top title in a beauty contest.

"I don't play games, sweetheart."

"Then what was that all about?" she demanded, sounding out of breath.

He smiled. "I was just telling an old friend good night."

She shook her head. "Good night is a handshake, a pat on the shoulder or a 'see you later.' It is not a kiss hot enough to blister paint."

Grinning, he rocked back on his heels. "So you thought my kiss was that hot, huh?"

"I didn't—" She stopped, then glaring at him, shook her head. "Stop trying to turn this back on me. You were the one who—"

Before she could get a good head of steam worked up, he took her back in his arms and kissed her until they both gasped for breath. When he raised his head, he was pleased to see her scowl had been replaced by a slightly dazed expression.

"Good night, Cheyenne. Drive carefully on your way home."

She stared at him for several seconds before she turned and without a word walked the distance to her truck.

As he watched the taillights of her truck disappear into the dark night, Nick took a deep breath and willed himself to relax. It appeared that convincing Cheyenne they could have a satisfying physical relationship was going to be easier than he'd first thought.

Turning toward the house, he climbed the steps and headed upstairs to a cold shower. He wasn't proud of the fact that he was consciously planning to seduce her. That really made him no better than his philandering father.

But his need for Cheyenne was a weakness that was too strong to resist. And as long as he made sure neither of them developed an emotional attachment, there was no chance of either of them getting in over their heads or being hurt.

Four

"You were out pretty late last night, princess." Bertram Holbrook rolled his wheelchair up to his place at the head of the kitchen table. "Did the auction run longer than usual?"

Cheyenne nodded as she opened the refrigerator to take out a carton of eggs substitute and a package of bacon. "There was a lot of stock being sold." She wasn't about to tell him that she'd also been detained at the Sugar Creek Ranch after the auction, who had detained her or why.

"Is the company looking to buy some more cattle?" he asked conversationally.

Unable to meet her father's questioning gaze, she busied herself arranging strips of bacon in a skillet. "I've been told that we're going to sell off these herds and bring in all new stock."

Her father frowned. "What's wrong with the cattle we have? Aren't Black Angus good enough for those corporate bigwigs?"

"There's nothing wrong with our stock." She turned to put bread in the toaster. "We'll still be raising and marketing Black Angus beef. But our herds will be free-range cattle."

"That's going to cost a small fortune to replace all those cattle. Why in the name of Sam Hill does the company want to do something like that?" He shook his head. "It looks to me like it would make more sense to use the stock they've got and just stop feeding them store-bought feed."

"There's a lot more to it than that, Daddy." She finished making their breakfast, then, setting a plate at each of their places, she poured them both a cup of coffee and sat down at the table across from him. "Besides, it's not my place to question what's planned for the Sugar Creek. My job is to follow orders and put the plan into action."

"That's the problem with these corporations trying to play around at being cattle ranchers," he said disgustedly. "They jump on the bandwagon every time something new comes along. Then they wonder why they aren't making money."

She shrugged. "Actually I think it's a good move. The market for free range beef is really growing right now and it doesn't look to stop any time soon. More people than ever are wanting their food to be raised naturally and that includes beef free of growth hormones and supplements."

He smiled. "You do make a pretty good argument, princess. If you think it's a good idea, then I'm sure it is."

They fell into silence as they ate and Cheyenne tried to think of a way to break the news to him that Nick Daniels was not only back in the area, he was the new owner of the Sugar Creek Cattle Company and the one responsible for changing the status quo. She knew that the longer she put off telling her father, the harder it would be.

For one thing, he wasn't going to be the least bit happy that Nick had returned. And for another, he was going to resent that she hadn't told him about it immediately. But his blood pressure and the possibility of another stroke had to be considered, too. If her father got upset, it could very well cause him more problems.

Lost in thought, it took a moment for her to realize that he'd asked a question. "I'm sorry. What was that, Daddy?"

"I asked if you saw anybody you knew at the sale barn last night."

Feeling more guilty by the second, she rose to her feet to clear the dishes from the table. "I wasn't all that happy about having to be there, so I really didn't pay that much attention. But I suppose the usual crowd was there."

Her father was silent for a moment before he quietly said, "I'm sorry, princess."

She turned to face him. "What for?"

"You shouldn't have to work so hard or be going places you don't want to go." The sadness etched in his once handsome face and the regret in his faded blue eyes broke her heart. "If I hadn't had the stroke, you'd be a schoolteacher instead of working off a debt that isn't yours."

Tears burned her eyes as she walked over and knelt down beside his wheelchair. "Oh, Daddy, please don't blame yourself. You couldn't help that you got sick. And I really don't mind ranch work." She smiled through her tears. "Remember what you told me when I was younger? You always said that I was the best cowboy you ever saw."

He put his arms around her shoulders and hugged her as close as the wheelchair would allow. "You're the best of everything in my life, princess. I don't know what I'd do without you."

She hugged him back. "I don't want you worrying about that because it isn't an issue. I'm taking care of everything."

Later that evening, as Cheyenne went about the task of feeding her gelding and Mr. Nibbles, the pony she'd had since she was five, then checked on a couple of calves she'd isolated because they'd shown signs of pink eye, she thought about what she had and hadn't told her father. She'd tried to be as honest as possible without telling him a lie. But dancing around the truth was getting more difficult with each passing day. And if that wasn't enough to have to contend with, the guilt of not telling him about Nick was weighing on her like a ton of bricks.

Sitting on a bale of hay outside her horse's stall, she weighed her options. Her father's health was frail at best and she didn't want to cause him any more problems. But she had four years left to work for Nick or Emerald, Inc. or whoever held her contract. And there was no way she could avoid telling him about Nick for that long.

She took a deep breath and started walking toward the house. Her father was having a fairly good day and the news might not affect him as badly as she feared, as long as she stressed there was no danger of her falling for Nick again. The only problem was, she wasn't sure who she'd be trying to convince of that fact—her father or herself.

But when she entered the kitchen, her heart plummeted. She could tell from the accusing expression on his face that he knew.

"I can't tell you how disappointed I am in you, princess. Why didn't you tell me that Daniels bastard is back?"

Instead of the remorse she expected, a huge sense of relief washed over her. "I'm sorry, Daddy. I didn't want to upset you and I wasn't sure how to tell you without doing that."

Her father sadly shook his head. "I would've rather heard it from you than learn about it from J. W. Schaefer."

"Was he at the auction last night?" she asked, not at all surprised that one of her father's acquaintances had seen her and Nick. Being a judge in a small county, Bertram Holbrook was well-known by nearly everyone, and so was his daughter.

"He was sitting a couple of seats away from you," her father said, nodding. "But that's not important. What I want to know is why Daniels is back here. And why were you with him? After the way he left here like a thief in the night thirteen years ago, I can't understand why you'd want to have anything to do with him."

Cheyenne hated having to tell him the rest of the

news. He was upset enough and she certainly didn't like the idea of upsetting him even more. But there was no way around it. He had to know everything.

"Nick is the new owner of the Sugar Creek Cattle Company, Daddy. He's my boss now. I don't have a choice."

He stared at her for several long seconds, then to her dismay, her father suddenly seemed to be much more calm. "Really? I wonder how he came up with the money for that?" He shook his head. "Did he give you any explanation about why he high-tailed it out of here all those years ago?"

Before she could answer that she had no idea, the phone rang. Answering on the second ring, she wondered how much worse her day could get when she discovered Nick on the other end of the line.

"Cheyenne, I know this is your day off and I'm really sorry about asking you this. But I need you to get over here right away." The urgency in his voice alarmed her.

"What's wrong?"

"I've got a mare in labor and she's showing signs of distress."

"Of course I'll help. Have you called Doc Connors? He's the veterinarian we've been using since Doc Haywood retired."

"Yes, but he's tied up at the McIntire ranch with

a possible outbreak of bovine tuberculosis and he's not sure when he'll be able to get here."

There was no hesitation in her answer. An animal was in trouble and it was her job as ranch foreman to see that it got the help it needed. "I'll be there in fifteen minutes or less."

When she hung up the phone, Cheyenne turned to her father. "I have to go help Nick with a pregnant mare having trouble giving birth."

Looking a bit distracted, he nodded. "Go ahead and do what you have to do, princess. I've been thinking about giving Gordon and a couple of my other cronies a call to see if they wanted to play cards this evening anyway."

As she gathered the first-aid kit she kept for animal emergencies around the ranch, her father proceeded to call Sheriff Turner and set up a game of poker. She thought it was a bit odd that her father had so readily dismissed the subject of Nick's return, considering how much he'd always disliked Nick. But Cheyenne didn't have time to speculate on her father's abrupt turnaround. The lives of a mare and her unborn foal were dependent on her doing her job. And that's exactly what she intended to do.

While Nick waited for Cheyenne to arrive, he got the agitated mare up and walking around the large birthing stall. He'd seen this type of problem before in other horses and although it had been a long time, he still remembered what to do when a foal's head failed to appear with both forelegs.

Sometime during the stage two phase of labor the foal had failed to position itself properly for the delivery. By getting the mare to walk, it would hopefully stop her from pushing and reduce the pressure on the foal. With any luck, the fetus would fall back into the womb enough to reposition itself for a normal birth.

"What seems to be the problem?" Cheyenne asked in a soft, low tone as she slowly approached the stall.

"We have a retention of the head," Nick answered just as quietly. Keeping the mare calm was crucial and any loud noise or sudden moves could increase her anxiety and cause more problems.

Easing into the stall, Cheyenne asked, "How long have you had her up and walking?"

"About forty-five minutes." He stopped the mare to check her hindquarters. "If the foal repositions, I think we'll be okay and have a normal birth. But if it doesn't present properly, I may have to reach inside and help."

Cheyenne stepped up to take hold of the mare's halter. "I'll keep her walking while you wash your arms with disinfectant."

As he walked down the wide center aisle of the

barn, Nick was thankful for Cheyenne's tranquil presence. She'd always had a way with animals and he was going to have to depend on her to help keep the mare calm in the event something intrusive had to be done.

When he stepped into the stall a few minutes later, Cheyenne was patting the horse's sweat-soaked neck and crooning to her softly. "She's tried to lie down several times, but I wanted to wait until you returned, in case she needs our help."

He nodded. "Let's get her down and see how it goes."

Without any encouragement from the two humans, the mare immediately lay down on her side on the thick bed of straw and began pushing to bring her colt into the world. Within minutes, first one tiny hoof, then the other emerged.

Nick found himself holding his breath, waiting to see if the foal's head presented as it should. When it did, he had to force himself not to let out a loud whoop of joy.

But his jubilation was short-lived when the mare suddenly relaxed as if her job was complete. Kneeling down beside her, he laid his hand on her belly. The contractions had stopped after the emergence of the foal's shoulders.

"Damn! I was afraid something like this would happen."

"She's too tired. I think you're going to have to help her." Worry was written all over Cheyenne's pretty face as she continued to pat the animal's sweat-soaked neck and he could tell she feared they'd lose both the foal and the mare. The same as he did.

He hadn't wanted to intervene if he didn't have to. But it appeared that the matter had been taken out of his hands. Nature wasn't going to take its course and he didn't have a choice.

Sitting behind the exhausted mare, Nick braced his boots flat on the floor of the stall for traction and, grasping the foal's fetlocks, slowly began to pull. He hoped the steady pressure of his efforts would restart the mare's abdominal contractions. But when it became apparent that it wasn't working, Cheyenne moved into position beside him without having to be told what to do and took hold of one of the foal's front legs.

"Ready?" he asked through gritted teeth.

When she nodded, they worked together and, careful not to injure the animal, they slowly began the arduous task of pulling the foal from the mare. Working for what seemed like hours, but in fact was only a matter of minutes, they finally succeeded and the new baby slid out onto the soft bed of straw.

While Cheyenne caught her breath from the physical exertion, Nick quickly cleared the bluish-white amniotic sac away from the foal's nose and muzzle. To his relief, the colt immediately moved its head and started breathing without further assistance, then rolled to its sternum to make the job a little easier. Turning his attention to the mare, Nick was further relieved to discover that, although exhausted from her ordeal, she appeared to be fine.

"We did it," Cheyenne said, throwing her arms around him.

They were still on their knees in the straw and her exuberant reaction damned near knocked him over, but he didn't care. He felt the same as she did. They'd seen the mare through the crisis and had good reason to celebrate.

"We sure did." Wrapping her in a bear hug, he pulled her close. "We make a hell of a team, sweetheart. If I hadn't had your help, I'd have probably lost both of them."

As he drew back to stare down at her, the feel of her soft body against his and the emotional bond they shared from having weathered the crisis together was too strong a connection to resist. Without thinking twice, Nick lowered his head to capture Cheyenne's lips with his.

Tunneling his hands through her glossy hair, the golden-brown strands flowed over his tanned skin like silk threads and the instant his mouth touched hers, an electric current traveled all the way from the top of his head to the soles of his feet. A need stronger than anything he'd ever experienced overtook him. He wanted her, wanted to lose himself in her sweetness and forget that they'd spent thirteen years apart or that they'd never have a future together. All that mattered was here. Now.

He leisurely savored her lips as he reacquainted himself with their softness. When Cheyenne splayed her hands across his back and pressed herself closer, the feel of her lush breasts crushed to his chest sent a shock wave straight to the most sensitive part of his anatomy.

She sighed at the contact and he instinctively knew she was experiencing the same intense need he was. Her acceptance of his kiss encouraged him and he slipped inside to taste the sweetness that was uniquely Cheyenne. Stroking her tongue with his, he teased and coaxed her into exploring him, but when she returned the favor, his heart thumped his ribs like a bass drum and the blood flowing through his veins felt as if it had been turned to liquid fire.

As she tentatively acquainted herself with him, it took everything Nick had in him not to take charge of the caress. But he sensed that she needed to feel in control, needed to come to terms with what he'd already accepted. They were going to make love. And, if their inability to keep their hands off of each other was any indication, it was going to be soon. The thought sent his hormones into overdrive and not only was his arousal immediate, the intensity of it left him feeling light-headed.

Unable to remain passive any longer, he tugged the tail of her T-shirt from the waistband of her jeans, then ran his hands along her sides to cup the underside of her breasts. When they were kids, he'd never taken the liberty of exploring her body, never touched her in any way that could have been considered inappropriate. But they were no longer teenagers and as far as he was concerned, there was nothing out of line between two consenting adults.

When he used his thumbs to tease her taut nipples through her lacy bra, her moan of pleasure vibrated against his lips and sent heat streaking to every cell of his being. "Does that feel good, Cheyenne?" he whispered.

She nodded. "We shouldn't be doing this."

"Do you want me to stop?"

"No."

He chuckled. "I shouldn't be touching you. But you don't want me to stop?"

"Yes…no…" She shivered against him. "I…can't think."

"It's okay, sweetheart." He rose to his feet, then pulled her up to stand in front of him. Staring at her upturned face, he smiled at the rosy blush of passion painting her porcelain cheeks. "I'm not going to lie to you. I want you, Cheyenne. I want to kiss every inch of your body, then sink myself deep inside you and watch you come apart in my arms when you find your release." He touched her satiny skin as he shook his head. "But I can't promise you anything beyond the pleasure. I'm not looking to start a relationship with you, nor do I want a commitment from you."

His lower body tightened further when her little pink tongue darted out to moisten her perfect lips. "In other words, you want sex with no strings attached?"

Put in such basic terms it sounded cold and calculating and he'd like nothing better than to deny it. But his conscience was stronger than his desire to finally claim her body.

"I didn't want to phrase it that way, but yes. That's exactly what I want."

Five

Even though she'd gotten over Nick years ago and the very last thing she wanted to do was become involved with him again, Cheyenne couldn't believe the level of desire that filled her at his admission that he wanted her. "I think I'll be going now. You should be able to handle things from here with the mare and colt."

He stared at her for several long moments before he nodded and stepped back. "Thanks for coming over to help. I really appreciate it."

Thankful that he wasn't going to pressure her, she shrugged as she knelt to repack the first-aid kit. "No need to thank me. Taking care of the Sugar Creek livestock is part of my job description." When she stood up and walked to the stall door, he started to follow her, but she shook her head. "There's no need for you to show me out. I know the way."

Needing to put distance between them, but unwilling to let him see how tempted she'd been by his confession, she forced herself to walk slowly from the barn and over to where she'd parked her truck. She felt Nick's gaze following her as she put the first-aid kit in the back, then opened the driver's door and climbed in behind the steering wheel.

As she started the engine and drove from the ranch yard, she had mixed emotions about what Nick was proposing. On the one hand, she didn't want a relationship with him any more than he wanted one with her. She'd suffered the sting of his rejection once. She certainly didn't want to spend years trying to get over him again. But on the other hand, whether she liked it or not her body craved his touch and she wanted him as badly as he wanted her.

She slowed the truck to a stop and, taking a deep breath in an effort to settle her frayed nerves, stared out the windshield at the quiet, starless night. She couldn't believe she was even considering his outrageous suggestion. But the truth of the matter was, she was tired of always doing the right thing, of always being the person someone told her she should be. Just once she'd like to throw caution to the wind and do something completely out of character, simply because it was what she wanted to do, instead of what everyone expected of her.

But could she have an affair with Nick without endangering her heart in the bargain? Was it possible for a woman to share her body with a man and not become emotionally attached? Did she even have the courage to try?

Cheyenne wasn't sure how long she sat there waging her internal debate or when she came to a decision. But before she had the chance to change her mind, she steered the truck back onto the road and drove back to the Sugar Creek ranch.

What she was about to do was the most impulsive, insane thing she'd ever done in her entire life. But it was too late to back out now. When she pulled her truck to a stop, Nick was still standing in the open doorway of the barn and from his seductive expression she could tell he knew exactly why she'd returned.

Suddenly unable to find the courage to get out of the truck, she was aware that he had started walking toward her. The closer he got, the faster her pulse raced and when he opened the door and took her hand in his to help her down from the seat, her heart skipped several beats.

Neither spoke as they walked the short distance to

the house and climbed the porch steps. But when they entered the foyer, Cheyenne stopped.

"Your housekeeper and her husband—"

"Live in the foreman's cottage down the road." He gently cupped her cheek with his callused palm and gave her an encouraging smile. "I promise we're alone, Cheyenne."

A tiny shiver coursed through her at the sultry look in his hooded blue gaze as he once again took her hand in his and led her upstairs to his bedroom. But instead of stopping beside the bed, he led her into the master bathroom.

"We're going to take a shower together," he said, removing her ball cap, then the elastic band holding her ponytail. He threaded his fingers through her hair as he lowered his head to hers. "Then I'm going to give you more pleasure than you've ever imagined."

Tender and soft, his kiss warmed her to the depths of her soul and as his mouth moved over hers, she refused to think of the possible consequences of her actions or that she was playing a fool's game with a man she couldn't trust. At the moment, all she wanted to do was feel his hard body pressed to hers and taste the passion on his firm male lips.

When he coaxed her to open for him, she readily complied and the feel of his tongue stroking hers sent a flash fire racing to the pit of her belly and caused every cell in her being to tingle to life. Wanting to get closer to him, she wrapped her arms around his waist and splayed her hands over the firm muscles of his broad back.

It didn't matter that Nick was the last man she should be kissing or that her decision could very well be the biggest mistake of her life. She was too caught up in the feel of his strength surrounding her, his hands molding her to him and his strong arousal pressed to her lower abdomen.

Her heart pounded against her ribs and her mind began to spin when he broke the kiss and, holding her gaze with his, slid his hands from her back to her sides, then up under the tail of her T-shirt to pull it over her head. He tossed it to the floor, then made quick work of unfastening her bra.

His gaze never wavered as he drew the straps from her shoulders and she shivered in anticipation of his touch. Heaven help her, but she wanted to feel his hands on her, wanted him to explore her in ways that she'd never experienced before.

But just when she thought he was going to caress her heated body, he took a deep breath and knelt to remove their boots and socks. When they were both barefoot, he reached to unbuckle her belt. He seemed to be devoting his total concentration on each task and not once did he look at her body.

Once he had the leather strap unfastened, he pushed the button through the buttonhole, then slowly eased the zipper down. Her heart pounded so hard, she was surprised it didn't leap out of her chest when he hooked his thumbs in the elastic at the top of her panties and eased them and her jeans down her legs.

When he straightened, his blue gaze seemed to touch her everywhere and instead of feeling the self-consciousness she'd expected, she felt more feminine than she'd ever felt in her life. "You're even more beautiful than I imagined, Cheyenne." Smiling, he guided her hands to the snaps on the front of his chambray shirt. "Your turn, sweetheart."

Her fingers trembled as she slowly opened each one of the metal closures and when she finally parted the garment to push it from his wide shoulders, her breath caught. When they'd been teenagers, she'd seen him without a shirt and thought he had a nice physique. But the lanky body of the eighteen-year-old boy she'd known had grown into the impressively muscular body of a man. And he was absolutely gorgeous.

As she unbuckled his belt and reached for the snap at the top of his jeans, the sight of his bulging fly had her hastily amending her assessment of him. Not only did Nick have an impressive body, but he was the perfect specimen of a thoroughly aroused man in his prime. The room suddenly felt several degrees warmer and she couldn't seem to get her fingers to work.

"I think you'd better do this," she finally said, surprised that her voice sounded a lot more steady than she felt.

The sexy sound of his low chuckle sent a wave of longing straight to the pit of her belly and made her knees feel as if they had been turned to rubber. "You're probably right. Metal zippers can be damned dangerous to a man in my condition."

Watching Nick carefully pull the zipper down, then push his jeans and white cotton briefs down his muscular thighs caused tiny sparks of electric current to skip over every nerve in her body. When he kicked his clothes aside and she caught a glimpse of his magnificent body, her heart stalled. His chest wasn't the only impressive part of his superb physique.

"You're perfect," she said aloud.

He shook his head and pulled her into his arms. "Not as perfect as you."

The contact of feminine skin with hard male flesh and the feel of his strong arousal pressed to her soft lower belly sent the tingling sensation racing to her very core.

"You feel so damned good, sweetheart." His deep voice was rough with desire and caused an answering shiver of compelling need to slide over every inch of her.

When she finally managed to draw a breath, she nodded. "So…do you."

Caught up in the delicious sensations swirling throughout her body, she wasn't sure when Nick turned on the water and moved them under the warm spray. But the feel of water sliding over her sensitized skin helped restore some of her sanity.

She'd never in her life showered with anyone and until that moment, she'd never considered how intimate it could be. If he'd given her the opportunity, she might have even been a little embarrassed by how truly exposed she was. But Nick didn't give her the chance.

Turning her away from him, he poured a dollop of shampoo into his hands and began to work it into her long hair. His fingers felt wonderful massaging her scalp and any traces of apprehension she might have had disappeared immediately.

When he rinsed her hair, he gave her a quick kiss before washing and rinsing his own. Then, taking a bar of soap, he worked it into a lather and began to slide it over her shoulders and collarbone. Placing it in the built-in soap dish, he slowly ran his soapy hands up along her ribs to cover her breasts. The friction of his palms caressing her, the calluses chaf-

ing her pebbled nipples sent ribbons of desire thread-
ing their way throughout her body.

As he leisurely smoothed his hands over her upper
torso, Cheyenne closed her eyes and reveled in the
delicious sensations coursing through her. Massaging
her everywhere he touched, Nick created a need
within her like nothing she'd ever known before. And
by the time he reached her lower belly, she was certain she'd go completely mad from the intense longing building deep inside of her.

"You're making me crazy," she said, turning and
bracing her hands on his wide chest.

"Trust me, sweetheart. It's only going to get better."

His mouth came down on hers with an urgency
that stole her breath and she eagerly returned his kiss
with a boldness that might have shocked her if she'd
been able to think about what she was doing. But
with the tantalizing fog of passion clouding her mind
and his hands slowly skimming the insides of her
thighs, all she could do was feel.

At the same time as he slipped his tongue inside
to stroke her tender inner recesses, he placed one
arm around her back to steady her, then used his
other hand to part the delicate folds of her feminin-
ity. Sparkles of light danced behind her closed eyes
and her knees threatened to give way at the exquisite
tightening in her womb.

Just when she thought she'd go into total melt-down, he gently broke the kiss and, putting a bit of space between them, handed her the soap. "I scrubbed your back, now it's your turn to scrub mine."

Cheyenne realized that in slowing down his sensual exploration, he was actually heightening her anticipation of things to come. Taking a deep breath, she smiled as she ran the bar of soap over his heavily muscled chest and rippling stomach.

"I don't know how to tell you this, cowboy. But you need a lesson in female anatomy if you think that was my back."

His sexy grin caused her stomach to flutter. "I'll tell you what. I'll teach you about the male body, if you'll teach me about a woman's."

Her heart skipped several beats when he took the soap from her. She'd bet her next paycheck that he knew a lot more about the female form than she knew about a man.

"Lesson number one," he continued, guiding her hand to him. "This is what you do to me, how much you make me want you."

At the same time as her fingers encircled his engorged flesh, Cheyenne watched his jaw tighten and his eyes close a moment before he shuddered against her. An overwhelming sense of feminine power overtook her as she explored his body. Testing the strength and weight of him, she had no doubt about the depth of his desire for her.

He suddenly opened his eyes and caught her hands in his to hold them to his chest. "I think we'd better dry off and take this to bed while I still have the strength to walk."

Turning off the shower, he dried them both with fluffy towels, then giving her a kiss so tender it brought tears to her eyes, he picked her up and carried her into the bedroom. When he set her on her feet beside the bed, she pulled the comforter back and lay down while he turned on the bedside lamp and removed a foil packet from the nightstand.

She caught her lower lip between her teeth to keep it from trembling as she watched him place the condom under his pillow. She was nervous, but her anxiety had nothing to do with having second thoughts and everything to do with her inexperience. But when Nick stretched out beside her, then gathered her to him, her apprehension was quickly forgotten as the feel of his strength overwhelmed her.

His mouth touched hers in a feathery kiss. "I wanted to take this slow, but I'm so damned hot for you, I'm not sure that's going to be an option."

Before she could respond, his lips claimed hers and his need, the taste of his passion sent pleasure racing to every cell of her being. As his tongue swept over her mouth, then darted inside to stroke her, she savored his hunger and reveled in the excitement building deep within her.

When he slid his callused palm along her side, then caressed her breast, a heavy coil of need settled in the pit of her stomach and she couldn't stop a frustrated moan from escaping on her ragged sigh. Wanting to touch him, to explore his incredible body the way he was exploring hers, Cheyenne placed her hands on the thick pads of his pectoral muscles. His flat male nipples puckered in response and his groan of pleasure rumbled up from deep in his chest.

He nibbled kisses along the column of her throat to her collarbone, then down the slope of her breast, causing her breath to come out in tiny little puffs. But as his mouth closed over the hardened peak, the sensation of his warm, wet tongue on her sensitized skin had her wondering if she would ever breathe again.

"You're so soft...so sweet," he murmured as he slowly moved his hand down her abdomen to the juncture of her thighs.

She gasped when he parted her, then teased her with a gossamer touch. The tightening deep inside her lower belly increased tenfold and she couldn't seem to lie still.

"Nick, please!"

"Easy, sweetheart," he whispered as he continued

to tease the tiny nub of intense sensation. "I'll take care of you."

A tremor passed through her and she caught her breath at the empty ache forming in her lower body. "I need…please—"

His kiss was so tender, so poignant she felt as if she would melt. "Do you want me, Cheyenne?"

"Yes."

"Now?"

"Yes."

"Where?"

She was quickly losing her mind and all he could do was ask questions?

"Please…I need you…inside."

He raised his head and gave her a smile filled with the promise of things to come before he reached beneath the pillow for the foil packet. Her heart raced and her breathing became shallow as she watched him arrange their protection.

But when he nudged her knees apart, then settled himself over her, she closed her eyes and braced herself for whatever happened next.

"Look at me, Cheyenne."

When she did as he commanded, he held her gaze with his as he guided himself to her, then slowly, carefully pushed his hips forward. The exquisite pressure she felt as her body stretched to accommodate him was indescribable and instead of the pain she expected, her entire being hummed with a longing to be completely filled by him.

Nick could have never in his wildest dreams imagined the incredible degree of hunger that Cheyenne instilled in him. It was as if he'd finally found the other half of himself when he fitted his body to hers to make them one.

But as he savored the feeling, his heart suddenly stalled and he went completely still at the barrier he met within her. "What the hell—"

The unusual tightness surrounding him, the unexpected resistance and the flash of pain clouding her aqua eyes could only mean one thing. Until that moment Cheyenne had never been with a man.

"You're a virgin," he said, careful to hold his lower body perfectly still.

"Not…anymore." She gave him a tremulous smile. "I'm pretty sure…you just took care…of that…issue," she said breathlessly.

"But you're twenty-nine."

"And you're thirty-one." She grinned. "But I don't think either of us is ready for social security just yet."

"You've never done this before." He knew he wasn't making a hell of a lot of sense. But he was having the devil of a time believing that in the past thirteen years she hadn't found someone she wanted to be with. At least once.

"Does that make a difference?" she asked, suddenly sounding defensive.

Gathering her to him, he smiled as he kissed her stubborn little chin. "No, sweetheart. It doesn't make a damn bit of difference. I just wish that you had told me, that's all."

"Why?"

"Because if I hadn't been trying to take things slowly and make this last, I could have hurt you more than I did."

His body demanded that he complete the act of making her his, but he gritted his teeth and did his best to ignore it. Cheyenne needed time to adjust to the changes caused by his invasion.

She reached up to touch his cheek with her delicate hand. "I'm fine. Really."

"Are you sure?" Her eyes had softened and her body had relaxed some, but he needed to make sure.

When she nodded, he slowly pulled back, then moved forward, ever watchful for any sign of her discomfort. Detecting none, he set a slow pace and all too soon he felt himself climbing the peak of fulfillment.

Unwilling to complete the journey without her, Nick reached between them to lightly caress her fem-

Play the
Lucky
Hearts *Game*

and get...

2 FREE BOOKS
and a FREE MYSTERY GIFT...
yes! YOURS to KEEP!

I have scratched off the silver card.
Please send me my *2 FREE BOOKS* and
FREE mystery GIFT. I understand that I am
under no obligation to purchase any books as
explained on the back of this card.

Scratch Here!
then look below to see
what your cards get you...
2 Free Books & a Free
Mystery Gift!

326 SDL EEXW   225 SDL EEWM

FIRST NAME	LAST NAME

ADDRESS

APT.#   CITY

STATE/PROV.   ZIP/POSTAL CODE   (S-D-02/06)

Twenty-one gets you
2 FREE BOOKS
and a *FREE MYSTERY GIFT!*

Twenty gets you
2 FREE BOOKS!

Nineteen gets you
1 FREE BOOK!

TRY AGAIN!

The Silhouette Reader Service™ — Here's how it works:

BUSINESS REPLY MAIL

FIRST-CLASS MAIL   PERMIT NO. 717-003   BUFFALO, NY

POSTAGE WILL BE PAID BY ADDRESSEE

SILHOUETTE READER SERVICE
3010 WALDEN AVE
PO BOX 1867
BUFFALO NY 14240-9952

NO POSTAGE
NECESSARY
IF MAILED
IN THE
UNITED STATES

inine secrets. Her immediate tightening around him indicated that she was reaching for the summit and, deepening his strokes, he held himself in check as she found her pleasure and came apart in his arms.

Only then did he unleash the tight control he'd struggled to maintain and give in to his own release. He hoarsely whispered her name as he thrust into her one final time and felt the triumphant of completion as he emptied himself deep inside her tight body.

Several moments later, when he found the strength to lever himself away from her, he rolled to the side and gathered her into his arms. "Are you all right?"

"I can't believe how incredible that was." The awe in her soft voice reassured him that she hadn't found the experience as unpleasant as he'd feared it might be after learning it was her first time.

"I promise that next time will be even better," he said, kissing the top of her head.

She snuggled closer. "I don't see how that's possible."

Chuckling, he leisurely ran his hands over her satiny skin. "Just give me a minute or two to recover and I'll show you."

They lay in companionable silence for several long moments before she raised up to glance at the clock on the nightstand. "Oh, dear heavens! I didn't realize it was so late."

She started to pull from his arms, but Nick held her close. "What's your hurry, sweetheart?"

"I need to get home."

He brushed his lips over hers. "Spend the night with me, Cheyenne."

"I can't. I have to get home to see about my father. He'll be worried." When she tried to get up a second time, Nick let her go.

As he watched, she scurried into the bathroom and when she emerged a couple of minutes later she was fully dressed.

Rising from the bed, he removed a fresh pair of jeans from his closet and pulled them on. "I'll walk you out to your truck."

"There's no need." Her expression was unconcerned as she shrugged one slender shoulder. "That's the beauty of a 'no-strings' arrangement. You don't have to observe the conventions of a relationship."

"Maybe so, but that doesn't mean a man shouldn't be a gentleman about things," he growled. It was completely ridiculous, but her words irritated the hell out of him. "Besides, I want to kiss you good-night."

Her smile sent his blood pressure soaring. "A simple kiss was what got all this started in the first place."

Placing his arm around her shoulders, he walked her down the stairs and out onto the front porch. "If

I kiss you again, will you reconsider spending the night with me?"

"No."

He kissed her until they both gasped for breath. "You're sure?"

She looked a little dazed as she started down the porch steps. "Right now, I'm not even sure of my own name."

"Good night, *Cheyenne,*" he said, laughing.

As he watched her truck disappear down the lane, Nick leaned his shoulder against the newel post and stared up at the night sky. Nothing would have pleased him more than to spend the night with her, then wake up tomorrow morning with her in his arms.

When his body tightened at the pleasant thought, he shook his head to clear it. "That doesn't sound like a no-strings affair," he muttered, suddenly disgusted with himself.

Walking back into the house, he headed straight for the bathroom and a cold shower. How the hell could he still burn for her after the most incredible sex of his life?

But some time later, as he lay shivering in his empty bed, Nick was still having a problem wrapping his mind around the idea that up until a couple of hours ago, Cheyenne had still been a virgin. Surely she'd had other boyfriends after he left Wyoming— if not in high school, at least in college.

Why had she waited until now to lose her virginity? Hadn't she found a guy in the past thirteen years that she'd had special feelings for?

When they'd been teenagers, she'd certainly given every indication that she'd thought he was that special. But out of respect for her and not wanting to be anything like the man who'd spawned him, Nick had been determined to make Cheyenne his wife first.

With his heart racing, his body jackknifed and he sat straight up in bed. Had she waited all this time because she hadn't felt as close with any other man as she had with him? Did she still feel that way?

His mind reeled from the implications. Earlier, in the barn when he'd laid his cards on the table and told her up-front that he didn't want a relationship with her, but that he did want them to have sex, she hadn't been able to get away from him fast enough. But not fifteen minutes later, she'd come back and accepted his terms. Then, after honoring him with the gift of being the first man to touch her, of making the most amazing love with him, she'd reminded him theirs was a no-strings affair.

Collapsing back against his pillow, Nick shook his head. How the hell was a man supposed to understand what was going on when he was getting such mixed signals? And why was he letting it get to him?

He hadn't come back to Wyoming to take up

KATHIE DeNOSKY 101

where he left off with Cheyenne Holbrook, nor did he want to. Unbeknown to him, his mother had requested that after her death Emerald hold his land in order for him to reclaim it when she decided he was ready. That's why he'd returned and that's exactly what he intended to do.

Besides, he and Cheyenne were two different people now and it was best the way things had turned out. The likelihood of them sharing anything more than a few laughs over old times and some really amazing sex was slim at best.

After all, he was Owen Larson's son and he'd proven time and again that relationships weren't his strong suit. It was probably just a matter of time before he lost interest in Cheyenne and the last thing he wanted to do was hurt her.

He frowned as he stared up at the ceiling. But she seemed to be doing all right with their arrangement—maybe even better than he was. He couldn't believe the level of irritation that ran through him when she'd told him that he didn't have to walk her out to her truck. But that was probably due to her inexperience with the dynamics of a no-strings affair. She didn't realize that whether emotions were involved or not, after a woman shared her body with a man, she deserved to be treated like a lady.

Satisfied that he had it all figured out and once

again had his priorities straight, he turned to his stomach and concentrated on getting a good night's sleep. But instead of ways to improve the ranch or the new free-range program he intended to start, his last thoughts before he went to sleep were of making love to a beautiful girl with long golden-brown hair and aqua eyes named Cheyenne.

Six

"**D**addy, did you hear anything unusual after I got home last night?" Cheyenne asked her father as she came in from outside.

When her father looked up from the crossword puzzle he'd been working, he shook his head. "No, why, princess?"

"Because I have four flat tires on my pickup truck." Walking straight to the phone, she punched in the number for the county sheriff's office. "And it looks like someone used an ice pick to puncture holes in the side walls."

His expression indignant, he slapped his puzzle

book down on the table. "Who in tarnation would have the nerve to come onto my property and do such a despicable thing?"

Cheyenne held up her index finger to silence his outburst when the county dispatcher picked up on the other end of the line. "Wilma, this is Cheyenne Holbrook. Could you please send a patrol car out to the Flying H Ranch? I'm afraid we've had some trouble with vandals."

"Cheyenne, honey, are you and your dad all right?" the woman asked anxiously.

"We're fine. But I can't say the same for my truck." Cheyenne sighed. "I have four tires that resemble Swiss cheese."

"I'll send Gordon out right away to take your statement and fill out a report."

Cheyenne cringed at the sound of the sheriff's name. She'd never liked Gordon Turner and the less she had to do with him the better. "That's not necessary, Wilma. Just send one of the deputies."

"Good heavens, Cheyenne. Are you looking to get me fired? Gordon is going to insist on taking care of this himself since it happened out there at the judge's ranch."

The woman immediately turned away to radio the sheriff. When she came back on the line, Wilma announced, "He says he'll be there in about twenty minutes."

Sighing, Cheyenne thanked the woman, then hung up the phone. For the sake of her father's pride very few people knew that they were no longer the owners of the Flying H. She supposed having to deal with Sheriff Turner was a small price to pay to keep her father's dignity intact.

"Is Gordon on his way?" her father asked, backing his wheelchair away from the table.

She nodded. "Wilma said he should be here in a few minutes."

Her father waved his hand toward the door. "Push me out onto the back porch. I want to make sure he knows who to question about this trouble."

She pushed his wheelchair out onto the covered porch, then locked the wheels. "We've never had this kind of problem before. Why would you think you know who punctured my tires when I can't think of a soul who would do something like this?"

"Think about it, princess. We've never had trouble like this before." He pointed to the west. "But Nick Daniels moves back into the area and in sight of a week you have four flat tires. Didn't I always tell you he was nothing but bad news?"

Shocked by his vehemence, she shook her head.

"No, Daddy. I don't think so. What would Nick gain by vandalizing my truck?"

"He could be trying to get you to quit your job." Her father sounded a little less passionate, but no less convinced that Nick was guilty of the crime.

"If he didn't want me working for him, I'm certain Nick would tell me so and terminate my contract with the Sugar Creek Cattle Company."

"I'm not so sure about that," her father said stubbornly. "That boy was up to no good thirteen years ago and you can bet he's up to no good now. Once a troublemaker, always a troublemaker."

Cheyenne patted his shoulder in an effort to calm him down as they waited for the sheriff to arrive. She wasn't about to tell him that unless it was some kind of bizarre mating ritual no one ever heard of, she seriously doubted that Nick would flatten all four of her tires after making love to her so tenderly only a few hours before.

"Whatever you say, Daddy."

"I mean it, Cheyenne." He took hold of her hand. "There are things about that Daniels boy you don't know anything about."

His insistence and the earnest expression on his face unsettled her. "What are you talking about, Daddy? I don't remember—"

"You know I'm not at liberty to talk about the aspects of past cases, princess," he interrupted. "But believe me when I tell you, that boy is no good and never will be."

"Nick?"
Looking up from the ranch records, he smiled. "What can I do for you, Greta?"

"Cheyenne's here."

"It's about damn time. She's over three hours late."

At first, he'd wondered if she'd overslept. But the later it got, he'd started to worry that he might have hurt her more last night than she'd let on.

Standing up, Nick walked around the desk, but something about his housekeeper's frown stopped him dead in his tracks. "What's up?"

"Sheriff Turner is with her. They're in the great room." Greta lowered her voice. "Do you want me to call Carl?"

Nick had no idea why he was being paid a visit by Gordon Turner, but he was no longer an inexperienced teenage boy. He could fight his own battles and he damned well wasn't going to let the man run roughshod over him again.

"There's no need to call Carl, Greta. I can take care of whatever the sheriff wants."

He waited until the woman started back toward the kitchen before he crossed the hall into the great room.

"Sheriff Turner. Cheyenne." He nodded a greeting. "I'm guessing this isn't a social call."

Turner grunted. "Not hardly. Just where were you last night, Daniels? And what were you up to?" The sheriff's sanctimonious expression was meant to intimidate, but only served to make him look like a puffed-up bullfrog.

"I've already told you that Nick and I had to help a mare with a difficult birth," Cheyenne said, turning on the man.

Sheriff Turner shook his head. "I want to hear where he was after you left here to go home. And I want to hear it from him, not you, Ms. Holbrook." Turning back to Nick, he narrowed his eyes. "I'm waiting, Daniels."

Nick met the man's accusing glare head on. "I was right here all night."

"Is there someone who can verify that?"

"No. After Cheyenne left, I was alone the rest of the evening." Nick didn't like the sheriff's condescending attitude or the direction his questioning was headed. "Why do you ask?"

A vein began to throb at the man's temple. "I'm the one asking the questions here. All I want from you is answers."

"Oh, for heaven's sake. It's not like it's a state secret, Sheriff." Cheyenne looked angry enough to bite nails in two. "Someone punctured all four of my truck tires last night," she said, turning to Nick. "I tried to tell him that you had nothing to do with it, but he won't listen."

Sheriff Turner stubbornly folded his arms over his barrel chest. "The judge said to question Daniels here, and that's what I'm doing."

Anger, swift and hot welled up inside of Nick at the mention of the judge. It appeared that disabled or not, His Honor, Bertram Holbrook, still had Gordon Turner dancing to his tune.

"Are you accusing me of having something to do with the vandalism, Sheriff?"

"I didn't say that." Some of the sheriff's arrogance seemed to slip and he couldn't quite meet Nick's steady gaze. "I'm just trying to investigate what happened."

"I was here. Alone." Nick hardened his voice so there was no mistaking his meaning. "And unless you have evidence that says otherwise, I suggest you look elsewhere for whoever caused the trouble, because it wasn't me."

A dull flush colored Sheriff Turner's puffy cheeks. "I'll be watching you, Daniels. Don't think I won't." When he turned to leave, he motioned for Cheyenne to follow him. "Come on, Ms. Holbrook. I'll give you a ride back home."

Cheyenne shook her head. "I'll have Nick drive me home later."

"Your father—"

"Knows that I'll be home later," she said, glaring at the man.

The sheriff looked as if he wanted to argue the point, but when it was clear that Cheyenne was going to stand her ground, Turner wisely chose to leave without her.

"I'm so sorry about this, Nick," she said when they heard the front door close. "I tried to tell my father and the sheriff that I didn't think you had anything to do with the incident, but they wouldn't listen. They insisted that you needed to be questioned about it since you'd been in trouble before."

He frowned. Unless she was talking about the night they tried to elope, he'd never in his entire life done anything to land his ass in trouble with the law. And it didn't set well that after he'd moved to St. Louis he'd been falsely accused of doing things without the benefit of being there to defend himself.

"Would you like to refresh my memory? I don't seem to recall doing anything illegal. Just what was it that I was supposed to have done?"

She looked confused. "I'm not sure. Daddy said he couldn't talk about past cases. But I told him that I was sure if you had done something it couldn't have been anything more than a boyish prank."

Although he'd never been able to figure out why, Nick had always known the judge had no use for him. But he'd never dreamed the man would stoop so low as to make up a pack of lies about him.

More furious than he could ever remember, he chose his words very carefully. "Out of respect for you, I'm not going to call your father a liar, Cheyenne. But rest assured, I have never in my entire life broken the law. Not at eighteen. Not now."

"I don't…understand."

He could tell that his impassioned statement and the intensity in his voice startled her. He regretted that. But it couldn't be helped. It was past time for her to face facts. Everything she'd been led to believe about him had been colored by her father's hatred toward Nick's family.

But as much as he wanted to set the record straight, he needed time for his anger to cool. When he explained why he and his mother had left Wyoming in the dead of night, he fully intended to keep his head about him and his temper in check. None of it was Cheyenne's fault and he didn't want to leave her with the impression that he blamed her.

"Don't worry about it, sweetheart. We'll discuss it later." Taking her in his arms, he pressed a kiss to her forehead. "Do you have any idea how amazing you were last night?"

"Not really." He felt some of her tension ease away as he held her close. "I'm not sure…"

When he nibbled at the delicate hollow behind her ear, her voice trailed off. "Were you sore this morning?"

Her porcelain cheeks colored a pretty pink. "A little."

"I'm sorry, sweetheart." He hated that he'd caused her even the slightest discomfort. But he could damn sure see that it didn't happen again. "We'll have to wait a few days before we make love again."

"Don't you mean *have sex?*"

Leaning back, he frowned. "Same thing."

She shook her head. "Making love carries the connotation of an emotional attachment. Having sex is the coming together of two individuals for the purpose of mutual satisfaction." She pulled from his arms and started walking toward his office. "But I'm not here to argue semantics with you. I'm here to get some work done."

It made absolutely no sense, but Nick had the urge to punch something. What Cheyenne said was true. Theirs was an affair with no emotional involvement. That's what he wanted and that's what she was giving him.

But every time she reminded him of that fact it pissed him off. And for the life of him, he had no idea why.

By Friday afternoon, Cheyenne found it extremely hard to concentrate as she sat in Nick's office staring at the preliminary list of cattle to be taken to auction on Saturday night. She'd spent most of the week thinking about the tire incident and Nick's assurance that he'd had no part in it.

Her father and the sheriff continued to suspect he'd been responsible for the vandalism, but it really made no sense. For one thing, puncturing tires was more of a juvenile act than something a grown man would do. And for another, she couldn't think of a single thing that Nick would gain from it.

Her father insisted that Nick had been in trouble with the law when he was younger, and he'd never lied to her. But Nick had been very convincing when he'd sworn that he hadn't. And unless she counted him telling her when they were teenagers that he'd love her until his dying day, to her knowledge he'd always been truthful with her, too.

So who was she supposed to believe? A father who had always had her best interest at heart? Or the man who had captured her heart when she was sixteen and really never let it go?

Her breath caught and she had to swallow around

the sudden tightening in her throat. Did she still love him? Was that the reason she'd made the uncharacteristic decision to have an affair with him?

Glancing up, she looked at Nick sitting across the desk from her. In some ways he hadn't changed since they were teenagers and in others he seemed to be a entirely different person than he had all those years ago. There was an edge to him now, a strength that she hadn't noticed when they were kids.

When he'd talked to the sheriff, she'd been left with the distinct impression that Nick wasn't the type of man to start a fight, but he definitely wouldn't back down from one. And she'd bet every last thing she owned that whether it was a physical or verbal battle, he'd be the last man standing once the final punch had been thrown.

Coupled with the gentle way he'd always treated her, his commanding presence and take-charge attitude only added to his sex appeal. And it was no wonder she found him completely irresistible.

Suddenly feeling as if the walls were closing in on her, she stood up. "I'm going to take a break and get a breath of fresh air." When he looked up from the ranch's cattle registries, she added, "I'll be back in a few minutes."

"I could use a break, too." He rose to his feet and started around the desk, but to Cheyenne's relief the phone rang. When he checked the caller ID, he smiled apologetically. "I need to take this call."

"That's fine." Actually, it was more than fine with her. Her sole reason for taking a break had been to spend a few minutes alone to try to sort through her feelings. "I'll be on the porch when you're finished with your phone call."

As she walked out onto the front porch and sat down on the suspended wooden swing, she stared out at the mountains in the distance. What in heaven's name was she going to do?

She was caught in an impossible situation with no way out. She loved Nick—had always loved him. For years, she'd tried to tell herself that she'd gotten over him, that she'd only had a foolish schoolgirl crush she'd mistaken for love.

But now she knew that hadn't been the case. All he'd had to do was kiss her and she was right back where she'd been thirteen years ago. She'd given her heart to him then, and as much as she would like to take it back now, she couldn't. Unfortunately for her, he'd made it clear that he didn't want it now any more than he had back then.

Her breath caught at the futility of it all. If she had the money to pay the balance on the promissory note she'd signed with Emerald, Inc., she'd resign as foreman of the Sugar Creek Cattle Company and move her and her father as far away as possible. But she didn't have enough in her meager savings account to even pay the interest on the loan.

Biting her lower lip to keep it from trembling, she didn't see any way out of the situation. She was trapped for the next four years, listening to her father's constant reminder that the man she loved was no good and couldn't be trusted, and knowing there was no chance of Nick ever loving her in return.

She took a deep shuddering breath. He was, and always had been, her biggest weakness and she'd made a huge mistake in thinking she could settle for anything less than his love.

But was she strong enough to call a halt to their "no-strings" affair, then work with him day in and day out until she'd fulfilled her contract? Would she be able to walk away at the end of the four years without making a fool of herself? More importantly, could she hide her feelings for that long without him finding out the way she felt about him?

Deciding she didn't have a choice, she stood up. If she had any chance of surviving, she knew what she had to do. She had to end their physical relationship now or risk losing what little sanity she had left. And as long as he didn't kiss her, she should be able to carry through on her decision.

* * *

"I'm glad to hear you've finally gotten over passing out every time you see a needle, Hunter." Nick laughed as he listened to his older brother tell about the E.M.T. courses he'd been taking. Until a few weeks ago, he hadn't even known that he had two brothers. But after discovering that his mother wasn't the only woman his father had loved and left to face single motherhood alone, the bond forming between him and his brothers meant more to Nick than anything had in a very long time. "How much longer before you get certified?"

"If I can pass this damned course without having to deal with too many needles, I'll get my certificate in about two weeks. Then I have to get checked out to fly choppers again." Hunter sighed heavily. "I'm still not a hundred percent sure that I want to do this. I just don't trust Emerald not to have something up her sleeve with this medical evacuation service that she's not telling me."

"Yeah, the old gal has a way of omitting details and twisting facts to get us to dance to her tune," Nick said, thinking about the things she'd conveniently failed to tell him concerning the expansion of the Sugar Creek ranch.

"Caleb told me about the mess she's gotten you into. Do you have that straightened out yet?"

"No." Nick released a frustrated breath. "Emerald

hasn't returned my phone calls and old Luther is as noncommittal as ever."

Hunter chuckled. "I'm still wondering where she found that guy. He's definitely not normal."

"Not by a long shot," Nick agreed, laughing.

"I guess I'd better get back to studying about compound fractures," Hunter said, sounding less than enthusiastic. "Good luck getting things straightened out with your foreman's contract."

"Thanks. I have a feeling I'm going to need it." As an afterthought, Nick added, "I can't wait to see what Emerald has in store for you."

Hunter groaned. "If it's anything like what she's gotten you into, I think I'd just as soon quit now and save myself the hassle."

Nick couldn't help but laugh. "And miss all the fun?"

After finalizing plans with Hunter to fly down to Albuquerque in a couple of weeks to surprise their brother, Caleb, on his birthday, Nick hung up the phone and stood to go in search of Cheyenne. She'd probably have to find someone to take care of her father for a few days, but that could be worked out. He had every intention of taking her with him and he wasn't taking no for an answer.

He had no idea why it was suddenly important to him that she meet his brothers. The fact of the matter was, he really didn't want to know. He had a feeling he wouldn't be overly thrilled with what he discovered if he tried to analyze his reasoning.

"Some things are better left alone and this is one of them," he muttered as he opened his office door and walked right into Cheyenne. Catching her by the shoulders to keep her from stumbling backward, he laughed as he pulled her to him. "Whoa, sweetheart. Where were you headed in such a hurry?"

"I…need to talk to you about—"

"We'll talk later," he said, lowering his mouth to hers.

The feel of her petite frame pressed to his chest was more temptation than he could resist. It had been the better part of a week since they'd made love and with each passing day, his need for her had grown into an unbearable ache.

As he moved his lips over hers, blood surged through his veins and a spark ignited in his gut. Her soft, feminine body pressed to his sent heat coursing straight through him and a shockwave of desire directly to the region south of his belt buckle.

Caught up in the feel of her perfect lips beneath his and the rapidly building hunger overtaking every fiber of his being, it took a moment for him to realize that she was pushing against him. "Hey, where do you think you're going?"

"Greta—"

He tightened his arms around her. "Greta left right after lunch. She and Carl are going down to Denver to spend the weekend with their daughter and her family."

"W-we're…alone?" If he didn't know better he'd swear there was a hint of panic in her voice.

Deciding he'd imagined it, he kissed his way from her cheek down the slender column of her neck. When he raised his head to meet her wide-eyed gaze, he smiled. "All alone, sweetheart."

Seven

A momentary wave of panic swept through Cheyenne when Nick's mouth covered hers. But she quickly ceased thinking of why it was so important that she call a halt to their affair or the risk she was taking of losing what was left of her sanity. Nothing mattered but the fact that she was in his arms once again.

When he eased his lips from hers to capture her gaze with his, the heat in his deep blue eyes caused her insides to hum with an anticipation that robbed her of breath. "I want you, Cheyenne." Low and slightly rough, his voice wrapped around her like a warm velvet cape and sent a wave of goose bumps shimmering over her skin. "I want to sink myself deep inside you and make our bodies one."

She knew she was playing a dangerous game and there was a very real possibility of losing what was left of herself. But if all she could allow herself to have with him was this one final moment, she'd cherish the memory of what they shared, no matter how much heartache she suffered later. Right now, she needed to taste the desire in his kiss and feel the strength of his passion as he claimed her one last time.

"Make love to me, Nick."

Without a moment's hesitation, he swept her into his arms and carried her up the stairs to his bedroom. When he set her on her feet at the side of his bed, his sexy smile chased away the last shadow of her doubts and she knew in her heart she'd lost her internal battle the moment he'd touched her.

After bending to quickly remove their boots and socks, he straightened, giving her a look that threatened to melt every bone in her body. "As much as I want to make love to you, I need to know. Are you still sore, sweetheart?"

Her cheeks heated at his intimate question. "The soreness went away after a day or two."

"Do you have any idea how pretty you are when

you blush?" he asked as he removed the elastic band holding her ponytail.

"I've never associated embarrassment…with feeling attractive." Her pulse sped up and her breathing became shallow when he trailed his fingers down her throat to her collarbone.

"I think you're pretty when you're happy, sad, angry—" he lightly ran his fingers over her shoulders, then down her arms to catch her hands in his "—and I even think you're pretty when you're embarrassed." Smiling he brought her hands to his lips to kiss each one. "When we were young, I thought you were the prettiest girl I'd ever seen. Now that we're grown, I *know* you're the prettiest woman I've ever seen."

Before she could get her vocal cords to work, he placed her hands on his shoulders, then reached down to tug the bottom of her tank top from the waistband of her jeans. Slipping his hands beneath the hem, the calluses on his palms sent waves of delight straight to the core of her as he caressed her ribs and the underside of her breasts.

"Raise your arms for me," he whispered close to her ear.

When she did as he commanded, he swept the lavender garment over her head and tossed it to the floor. Then, cupping her cheek with one hand, he kissed her with a tenderness that brought tears to her eyes as he reached behind her with the other hand to make quick work of unfastening her bra.

"How do men…do that?" she asked, feeling more than a little breathless.

"Do what?"

"Unfasten a bra one-handed faster than most people can snap their fingers."

A frown marred his handsome face as he leaned back to look at her. "How do you know—"

"Girl talk with some of my friends."

His rich laughter made her warm all over as he tossed the scrap of lace on top of her tank top, then nibbled kisses from her ear around to her throat. "Never underestimate the talents of a man on a mission, sweetheart."

At the feel of his lips on her sensitized skin, Cheyenne closed her eyes and let her head fall back to give him better access. A tingling excitement began to course through her veins, heating every inch of her as it made its way to pool in the pit of her belly. When he used his tongue to soothe the fluttering at the top of her collarbone, then kissed his way down her chest to the slope of her breast, she felt as if she'd melt into a puddle at his feet.

Caught up in the delicious sensations Nick was creating deep within her soul, her heart skipped several beats when he took her nipple into his mouth to draw on it deeply. Certain she'd burn to a cinder at any moment, she gripped his shoulders as the pooling of need in her lower body intensified.

"Do you like that?" His moist breath against her breast felt absolutely wonderful.

"Mmm."

"I'll take that as a yes." Turning his attention to her other breast, he treated the hardened peak to the same delightful torture.

Wave after wave of desire washed over her and it came as no small surprise when she realized that Nick had unsnapped her jeans and lowered the zipper without her knowledge. Sliding her jeans and panties down her thighs, he quickly added them to the growing pile of her clothes on the floor.

"This isn't fair. I'm completely naked and you still have all of your clothes on," she said, reaching out to unfasten the metal snaps on his Western-style shirt.

Knowing it would be their last time together, she forced herself to go slowly, to savor and enjoy the exploration of his magnificent body. She wanted to memorize every moment, commit every detail of their lovemaking to memory.

As she unsnapped first one gripper, then another, she kissed every inch of newly exposed skin and by the time she parted his shirt, Nick looked like a man in pain. "I think you're killing me."

"Do you want me to stop?" She grazed his flat male nipples with the tips of her fingers and was rewarded by his low groan of pleasure.

"Hell no, I don't want you to stop."

The hungry look in his dark blue eyes encouraged her and pushing his shirt off of his broad shoulders, she tossed it aside, then placed her hands flat on his bare chest. His warm male flesh felt absolutely wonderful beneath her palms and as she mapped the ridges and planes of his muscular physique, he took several deep, shuddering breaths.

Smiling, she trailed her index finger down the shallow valley dividing his rippling stomach muscles. "Your body is so beautiful, so perfect."

"It can't hold a candle to the perfection of yours, sweetheart," he said, shaking his head as he cupped her breasts with his hands.

The feel of his thumbs lightly chafing her tight nipples as he gently caressed her fullness sent her temperature soaring. He continued teasing her and by the time she unbuckled his belt and reached for the stud at his waistband, her fingers trembled from a need deeper than anything she'd ever experienced. Working the metal button free, she paused as she toyed with the tab at the top of his fly.

"It appears that you might have a bit of a problem."

"You caused me to be like this, sweetheart." The smoldering heat in his cobalt gaze caused the butterflies in her stomach to go absolutely wild and sent a shiver of anticipation up her spine.

Slowly brushing her hand across the faded denim, she smiled when he sucked in a sharp breath. "I'm responsible for this?"

"Yeah." He leaned forward to nibble kisses from her shoulder, up her neck to just below her ear. "Now, what are you going to do about it?"

Carefully lowering the zipper, the sight of his arousal straining against his cotton briefs filled her with an irresistible urge to touch him. Running her index finger along the hard ridge, she felt a moment of panic when he jerked as if he'd been shocked with a jolt of electricity.

"Is that uncomfortable?"

"Sweetheart, if you don't get the rest of my clothes off…it's going to be damned near unbearable. Real quick."

Cheyenne couldn't get over how empowering it felt to know that she'd brought him to such a heightened state of need. "That wouldn't be good."

"No, it wouldn't."

The hunger in his steady gaze encouraged her and, sliding her hands beneath the elastic at the top of his briefs, she slid them and his jeans over his narrow hips and down his powerful thighs. When he stepped out of them, then kicked them aside, the sight of his fully aroused body caused her heart to stall.

Crooking his index finger, he gave her a sexy smile. "Come here."

When she stepped into the circle of his arms, the feel of woman against man, skin against skin from shoulders to knees caused a delicious shiver of anticipation to slide through every part of her. But when he cupped her bottom in his large hands and lifted her to him, a sizzling awareness swirled from the top of her head to the soles of her feet, leaving her slightly dizzy from its intensity.

The honeyed heat deep in the most feminine part of her quickly changed to the empty ache of unfulfilled desire and she couldn't have stopped a moan of frustration from escaping if her life depended on. "I need you. Now."

"Easy, sweetheart." His kiss was filled with pure male passion and awakened a yearning in her deeper than she'd ever dreamed possible.

By the time he broke the kiss, she felt as if she would go up in a blaze of glory at any moment. Nick must have experienced the same sense of urgency because he reached into the bedside table to remove a foil packet and quickly arranged their protection. Then, settling himself on the side of the bed, he guided her to straddle his lap.

"Put your legs around me," he whispered hoarsely as he lifted her to him.

When she did, she reveled in the exquisite stretching of her body as he slowly eased her down onto his aroused flesh. Closing her eyes, Cheyenne felt a completeness that she knew in her heart she could never feel with any other man as he joined their bodies and made them one.

"You feel…wonderful," she said, wrapping her arms around his wide shoulders.

"I was about to say the same thing about you." His voice sounded strained and she could tell he was holding himself in check, making sure she was ready before he continued.

Opening her eyes, she raised one hand to thread her fingers in his thick, dark blond hair. Her heart ached with the need to tell him how special he was to her, how much she loved him. But knowing he didn't feel the same, she swallowed back the words and chose to show him how she felt about him.

"P-please…make love to me, Nick."

His gaze held hers as without a word he guided her in a leisurely rocking motion against him. When he slowly increased the pace, her head fell back as wave upon wave of exquisite pleasure radiated over every cell in her body. His lips caressing the sensitive skin of her throat and collarbone escalated the building tension deep inside her and all too quickly, she felt her body begin to tighten as the coil of need prepared to set her free.

He must have sensed her readiness because he tightened his arms around her. "I've got you, Cheyenne. Let go, sweetheart."

If she'd been able to find her voice, she could have told him that she didn't have a choice, that her body demanded she turn loose and reach for the completion they both sought. But her release from the captivating spell overtook her and she was cast into a vortex of incredible sensation.

Quivering from the waves of satisfaction flowing to every corner of her being, Cheyenne felt Nick's body move within her one final time, then stiffen as he found his own shuddering liberation from the passionate storm. As she clung to him, they both made the journey to a place where they basked in the perfect union of two bodies becoming one heart, one mind, one soul.

Tears filled her eyes and she tightened her arms around him in an effort to make the moment last. But as she slowly drifted back to reality, she knew the time had come to end the madness. She only hoped she had the strength to carry through with her decision and tell him their affair was over.

Nick couldn't believe the myriad of emotions tightening his chest. The possessiveness he'd been battling since seeing Cheyenne the first day of his return to the Sugar Creek ranch had grown into a force he could no longer fight. And it scared the living hell out of him.

He'd been a damned fool to think he could engage in any kind of physical relationship with her and not form some sort of bond. But to his relief, she'd apparently been just as affected by their affair. It hadn't been lost on him that she'd stopped referring to their coming together as having sex and started calling it what it was—lovemaking.

His chest tightened further and he suddenly found it hard to breathe. Had he done the unthinkable? Had he fallen in love with her again? Had he ever really stopped loving her?

Thirteen years ago, he'd been an infatuated teenage boy with a case of raging hormones and an inherent sense of honor. And in his attempt to avoid being anything like his irresponsible father, he'd confused lust for love and decided they had to be married before he made love to Cheyenne.

That explained his feelings for her in the past. But what about the way he was feeling now? Was he once again mistaking lust for something deeper, something far more meaningful?

His heart pounded hard against his rib cage and he had to force himself to breathe. The last thing he needed right now was to complicate his life by falling for Cheyenne again.

Deciding it would be better to sort everything out later when he was alone and could think more clearly, he kissed her satiny cheek and concentrated on the present. "Any discomfort this time?"

She shook her head. "No."

"Good."

They sat holding each other for some time before she started to pull away from him. "What's your hurry?" he asked, tightening his arms around her.

"I need to…get home." The tone of her voice warned him that something had upset her.

He lifted her from his lap to sit beside him on the bed. But instead of snuggling against him, she quickly stood up and started gathering her clothes from the pile on the floor.

"What's wrong, sweetheart?"

Instead of answering, she hurried into the bathroom. When she came out a few minutes later, he was waiting for her. There was no way in hell she was leaving until she explained what the problem was.

Placing his hands on her shoulders, he shook his

head. "You're not going anywhere until you tell me what's going on."

"Nothing…everything."

She looked about two seconds away from crying and it twisted his gut into a painful knot to think he might have caused her distress. "Slow down and tell me what's bothering you."

"I can't do this again." Her voice was so soft and tremulous, he almost hadn't heard her.

His heart stalled. She'd said there was no discomfort, but had he unknowingly hurt her in some way?

"Are you all right?"

"Don't worry about me. I'll be fine." Her sad smile caused his gut to twist.

"Then what's wrong?"

A lone tear slid down her pale cheek. "You can't change what happened any more than I can." She wouldn't look him in the eye when she motioned toward his clothes on the floor. "Will you please put something on? It's very distracting to try holding a conversation with a naked person."

"What do you mean we can't change what happened?" Frowning, he turned her loose to reach for his jeans and briefs. "If I did something that's upset you, I'm sorry."

As he started pulling on his jeans, she walked out

into the hall. Turning back, the sadness in her aqua eyes just about tore him apart.

"It's not what you did, Nick. It's what you can't do."

"Dammit, Cheyenne, wait a minute. You're talking in riddles."

In a hurry to follow her, he struggled to get his fly zipped, then started after her. But the sound of the front door closing behind her stopped him halfway down the stairs.

He had no idea what had just happened or why, but he had every intention of finding out. Turning, he went back to his bedroom for his shirt, then sitting on the side of the bed to pull on his boots, he thought about what she'd said.

For the life of him, he couldn't figure out what she'd been talking about. What didn't she think they could change? And what was it that she thought he couldn't do?

If she'd been referring to what happened thirteen years ago, she was right. He couldn't change the past. But he could damn sure explain what happened that night and why he and his mother had left Wyoming under the cover of darkness.

But as much as he wanted to set the record straight once and for all, he decided to wait until they drove back from the auction tomorrow evening to tell Cheyenne the truth about that night. She was too upset right now to listen to what he had to say and he wanted her full attention when he told her the role her father and the sheriff had played in one of the darkest days of his life.

By the time Cheyenne parked her truck in front of her house, she had her emotions under control. But only just barely. She knew she'd handled the situation with Nick badly. But that couldn't be helped. She'd done the best she could under the circumstances and if he didn't realize that she was ending their affair, he'd figure it out soon enough.

He'd probably wonder why she'd changed her mind. He might even question her about it. But after a time, he'd accept that it was over and move on to find a woman who could keep her emotions in check. Considering that he didn't love her, that shouldn't take too long.

"You look tired, princess," her father said as she let herself into the house through the back door. He was sitting in his wheelchair at the kitchen table with several of his old case files spread out in front of him. Slipping several of the papers into a folder, he stacked them on his lap. "Aren't you feeling well?"

No. She wasn't sure she'd ever feel good again.

"I do have a bit of a headache, but it's nothing. I'll be fine."

His eyes narrowed. "You had to work close to that blackhearted excuse for a human being again today, didn't you?"

"Daddy, please." She rubbed her throbbing temples. "I'm really not up to another lecture on how reprehensible you think Nick is."

His expression hard, he shook his head. "I just hate that you have to work for that illegitimate son of a—"

"Daddy!"

His features softened a bit. "I'm sorry, princess. But you're too good to be anywhere near Daniels, let alone have to work for him."

She knew her father only wanted the best for her and found the entire situation extremely frustrating. But neither one of them could change the fact that she had four more years on her contract with the Sugar Creek Cattle Company and there was no sense in belaboring the issue.

"Please, let's not talk about it now." She moved to take the files from him. "Do you want me to put these in your office?"

To her surprise, he held on to the files and shook his head. "Sit down and put your feet up. I'll put these back in the file cabinet, then we can talk about driving down to the Bucket of Suds Bar and Grill for supper. My treat."

"But I'd planned on making a meat loaf," she said

halfheartedly. She really didn't feel like cooking, but she hated for her father to use what little spending money she gave him each month on her.

"We can have meat loaf another time." He turned his wheelchair around and started rolling it toward his office. "You deserve a night off."

Two hours later, as she and her father sat at a chipped Formica table at the back of the Bucket of Suds, enjoying plates piled high with spaghetti and meatballs, Cheyenne felt as if the world had come to a grinding halt when Nick walked through the entrance. Hadn't she suffered enough turmoil in her life for one day? What on earth was he doing here? And what would her father do if he saw Nick?

As she stared at him, her chest tightened. She loved him so much she ached with it. And seeing him day in and day out without being held by him, loved by him was going to make the next four years drag out like a life sentence.

"Princess, did you hear what I said?"

Turning her attention to her father, she shook her head. "I must have been daydreaming."

"I said we should eat out like this more often." He smiled. "It feels good to get out of the house for a while."

She was glad to see that her father was enjoying his night out. Because of the demands of her job, she didn't have a lot of time to take him places and she knew he had to get bored staying at home all the time. She just hoped that he continued to enjoy himself and didn't recognize Nick. Fortunately the restaurant was packed with the usual Friday night crowd and the chances of that happening were fairly good.

Keeping an eye on Nick sitting at the bar, she did her best not to let on that anything was out of the ordinary. "I don't think our budget will allow us to eat out every week, but I think we can afford to do this once a month," she said, smiling.

Her father nodded. "It's something we can look forward to."

Aware of every move Nick made, Cheyenne knew the second he rose from the bar stool and headed toward their table. She tried to dissuade him with a surreptitious shake of her head, but she could tell by the determined look in his eye her effort was futile.

He nodded a greeting as he passed their table on his way to the jukebox. "Good evening, Judge Holbrook. Cheyenne."

"Who is that young man?" her father asked. "He looks familiar."

Cheyenne took a deep breath. "That was Nick Daniels, Daddy."

Her father's congenial expression quickly changed to a glare. "What's he doing here?"

"Probably for the same reason we are. His house-keeper went to Denver for the weekend and I assume he's here to eat dinner."

She swallowed hard when she recognized the beginning notes of the song she and Nick had always called theirs in high school. Why had he chosen that particular song out of all the ones on the jukebox?

"Housekeeper?" her father interrupted her thoughts. "Where's his mother? Didn't she come back to Wyoming with that whelp of hers?"

"Linda Daniels passed away about twelve years ago, Daddy."

"Linda's gone?" She could have sworn she saw a hint of sadness cross his face. But just as quickly as it appeared, it was gone.

Deciding she'd only imagined the change in his demeanor, Cheyenne nodded. "Nick said she knew she didn't have long to live when they left here to go to St. Louis."

As he walked back toward the bar, Nick stopped at their table. "When you left this afternoon, I forgot to tell you that we'll start loading the cattle we're taking to auction after lunch tomorrow."

Before she could respond, her father slammed his fork down on the table. "It's a damn fool idea to be selling off good stock the way you're doing. Of course, you never did have a lick of sense."

"Daddy," Cheyenne warned. Creating a scene in a public place would make the day go from difficult to unbearable.

"It's all right, Cheyenne." Nick smiled, but it was anything but friendly. "Your father has a right to his opinion." Although he'd spoken to her, his gaze never wavered from her father's.

"If you've said your piece move on, Daniels. You're ruining my appetite." As an afterthought, her father added, "And from now on, unless my daughter is on the clock, I don't want you anywhere near Cheyenne. Is that understood?"

Nick shook his head. "In case you hadn't noticed, she's an adult now, Judge. Who she does or doesn't see is her call. Not yours."

The level of hostility between Nick and her father shocked her. "I think you'd both better calm down. This isn't the time or place to be having a conversation like this."

"I was leaving anyway." When Nick finally turned his attention her way, the heat in his sensual gaze robbed her of breath and sent a shiver of awareness all the way to her soul. "I'll see you tomorrow afternoon, Cheyenne."

As he walked away, her father continued his diatribe, but Cheyenne had no idea what he was ranting about. There had been a wealth of meaning in the look Nick had given her and there was no mistaking his intention.

He had questions and he wasn't going to rest until he had the answers.

Eight

By the time the auction was over the next evening and Cheyenne waited for Nick to collect the money from the sale of the cattle, she felt ready to jump out of her own skin. Her nerves were completely shot, and for good reason.

She and Nick had worked together the entire afternoon to get the cattle loaded in trailers and moved to holding pens at the sale barn, then sat together while the animals were auctioned off to the highest bidders. Neither of them had mentioned the run-in he'd had with her father the night before, nor had he asked her why she'd had a sudden change of heart about their affair. But that was about to change.

They had a little over an hour before they got back to the Sugar Creek ranch and the complete privacy of his truck for their conversation. There wasn't a doubt in her mind what they would be discussing or that it was going to be one of the longest drives of her life.

"Ready to go?"

Lost in thought, she jumped at the unexpected sound of Nick's voice only inches away. "As ready as I'll ever be."

He smiled as he tucked the check he'd received from the auction officials in his shirt pocket, then put his arm around her shoulders to walk her to his truck. "Would you like to stop somewhere for a bite to eat before we head back?"

The feel of his body pressed to her side sent a deep longing straight to her soul. "N-no. I need to get home."

The last thing she wanted was to prolong the time they spent together. The more she was with him, the stronger the temptation became to rethink her decision.

"You've worked hard today." Opening the passenger door for her, he lightly ran his index finger from her ear along her cheek to her lips. "I'm sure you're tired."

Her skin tingled where he touched her and it took every ounce of willpower she had not to lean toward him. "I'm used to it." She forced herself to ignore the longing that streaked through her and got into the truck. "It's my job."

He shook his head. "Not anymore. Remember? You'll be in the office and I'll be out doing the ranch work."

If he thought she was going to argue with him, he was mistaken. She'd worked for six long years out in all kinds of weather and an easier job in the comforts of a heated office in the winter and air-conditioned in the summer didn't sound at all bad. And as long as she was alone in that office, she might even manage to retain a scrap of what little sanity she had left.

When he walked around the front of the truck and got in behind the steering wheel the look in his eye warned her that the conversation she'd dreaded was about to begin. "Your father looked fairly healthy last night, considering that he's had a stroke."

She nodded. "I can't get him to see a doctor as often as he should, but he's recovered everything but the ability to walk."

They rode in silence for some time before Nick asked, "What did your father tell you about the night I left Wyoming?"

His question wasn't what she expected. She'd thought he'd want to know why she'd ended their affair.

"Daddy didn't tell me anything until he received

the news that you and your mother were no longer at the Sugar Creek. Why?"

"I figured as much."

Confused, she turned to look at him as he gunned the truck's powerful engine. "What is that supposed to mean?"

He took a deep breath and she could tell he was doing his best to hold his temper. "Before I tell you what really went down that night, why don't you tell me what happened after your father led you away from the church?"

Cheyenne had expected them to be discussing her father's behavior the night before and her decision to end their no-strings arrangement. She couldn't imagine why Nick wanted to talk about the events of thirteen years ago.

"I don't see the need to drag up the past," she said, shaking her head. "My father broke up our wedding and you left without even telling me goodbye. End of story."

The lights from the dashboard illuminated his face just enough for her to watch a muscle work along Nick's lean jaw. "That's not exactly the way it all unfolded that night, Cheyenne."

She shook her head. "It doesn't matter now."

"Yes, it does."

Sighing heavily, she thought back on the night

she was to have become Nick's wife. "After my father and the sheriff stopped our wedding, Daddy took
me home and that was it. We didn't talk about it, until
a couple of days later when he told me that you and
your mother had left the area."

"What did he say?"

There was no sense mincing words. He was well
aware of how her father felt about him. "Daddy
pointed out that if you had really cared anything
about me, you would have told me where you were
going or at the least, told me goodbye."

Nick's particularly nasty oath startled her. "I'll
bet he didn't bother telling you why we left, did he?"

"How could he? My father didn't know any more
about your leaving than anyone else."

His hollow laughter caused a chill to slither
straight up her spine. "That's where you're wrong,
sweetheart. Your father and the sheriff had firsthand
knowledge of why I left Wyoming."

She was becoming more than a little irritated by
his intimations that her father had something to do
with it. "Well, since everyone seems to know all about
it but me, why don't you fill me in on the big secret?"

Nick stared out the windshield for several long
seconds before he finally spoke. "After your father
and the sheriff put you in the patrol car and left me
standing there on the church steps, I drove home and

told my mother what happened. She wasn't any happier about our trying to elope than your father, but for different reasons. She told me if she knew anything about Bertram Holbrook that we hadn't heard the last of the incident." He cast her a meaningful glance. "And she was right."

A cold dread began to settle in Cheyenne's stomach. She could tell by the look on his face that the accusations Nick was about to make against her father were going to be ugly and hurtful.

Swallowing around the lump in her throat, she asked, "Just what was it that my father was supposed to have done?"

She watched Nick's hand tighten on the steering wheel. "Around midnight that evening, my mother received an anonymous phone call, telling her that your father was filing charges and that the sheriff would be out the next morning to arrest me for statutory rape."

Gasping, she shook her head. "I don't believe you. My father would never do something like that."

Nick steered the truck to the side of the road and turned off the engine. When he turned to face her, his anger was evident in the tight lines around his mouth and the sparkle in his deep blue eyes.

"Don't fool yourself, Cheyenne. Your father was a powerful judge, who, for whatever reason, despised me and my mother. And I had taken his underage daughter—his only daughter—across the county line to marry her."

"But—"

"He had the motive, the resources and the hatred to pursue the issue." His gaze caught and held hers. "Face it, Cheyenne. Your father had every intention of seeing that I rotted away in a jail cell for the better part of my life."

Her stomach churned and she felt as if she might be physically ill. "I-if what you say is true, then why didn't you stay and fight the charges?"

"Think about it, sweetheart. Your father knew the law inside and out. And he had plenty of people to see that his goal was accomplished." He smiled sardonically. "What chance do you think I would have had at getting a fair trial with one of your father's colleagues sitting on the bench?"

Her mind reeled from the implications of it all. If what Nick told her had actually happened, it would have ruined his life. But she couldn't believe her father would do something so vile, so vindictive.

Taking her hand in his, Nick shook his head. "You have to believe me. The last thing I wanted to do was leave you behind that night. But as my mother pointed out, I didn't have any other options. I either got the hell out of Wyoming while I could or stay and face a guaranteed prison sentence."

Tears filled her eyes as she struggled with what he'd told her. "Why didn't you call…or write to let me know what had happened?"

"I tried to get in touch with you, but your father made sure that didn't happen." He reached down to release her safety harness, then pulled her to his wide chest. "I called every day for a month, sweetheart. But your father always answered the phone and wouldn't let me talk to you, or the answering machine picked up. I left messages, but it's my guess that he erased them before you heard them. I also sent a few letters, but I doubt you ever saw them, either."

She numbly shook her head. "No."

His arms holding her so securely to him were a comfort, but she felt completely overwhelmed and needed to be alone to sort out everything. "I…" Her voice caught. "P-please take me home."

Apparently sensing her need to come to terms with what he'd told her, Nick kissed the top of her head, then releasing her, started the truck.

As they drove in silence through the quiet night, Cheyenne thought about everything Nick had said. What was she supposed to believe?

The man he had described was nothing like the kind, loving father she'd always known. And until that very moment, there had never been a time in her life that she doubted her father having anything but her best interest at heart.

But as much as she hated to admit it, what Nick said made sense. At the time of the incident, her father did have the power and connections to pursue charges against him. And after seeing her father's hostility toward Nick last night, she couldn't deny that it was a possibility.

Why had her father always had such a low opinion of the Daniels family?

She'd never known anyone nicer than Linda Daniels, and even though the woman had had Nick at a time when it wasn't as socially acceptable to be an unwed mother, no one in the area had seemed to care. No one, that is, but her father.

Could that be the reason her father had such contempt for Nick? Had he viewed Nick as less of a person because his mother hadn't married his father?

But that made no sense. Why should her father be bothered by Nick's illegitimacy when no one else was?

Deciding there were no easy answers, Cheyenne rested her head against the back of the seat and tiredly closed her eyes. She had no idea who or what to believe anymore.

One of the two men she loved with all her heart had deceived her. And it didn't matter whether it was her father or Nick, when she discovered the truth, she knew without a doubt that it was going to break her heart.

Nick cursed his carelessness as he parked his truck beside the house and got out to climb the porch steps. He should have known better than to try to stretch a section of barbed wire fence without both work gloves. But like a damned fool, when he'd driven up to the north pasture that morning and discovered that he'd lost one, he'd gone ahead and tried to do the work without the protection of the thick leather covering his hands. Now he had a deep gash in his left hand and the fence still needed to be repaired.

"Greta, you'd better get the first-aid kit," he called when he entered the house.

"What's wrong?" Cheyenne asked, walking out of his office. She stopped short and her face went deathly pale. "Oh, dear Lord! What happened?"

Glancing down at the bloodstains on the front of his shirt, he held up his hand. "I tangled with some barbed wire."

"Let me see." She gently took his hand in hers and carefully unwrapped the blood-soaked handkerchief he'd wrapped around the wound. Looking up at him, she shook her head. "This is more than a scratch, Nick. Why weren't you wearing your gloves?"

Her soft hands holding his almost made him forget how much the gash hurt. "I could only find one of them and didn't want to drive all the way back here to get another pair."

Rolling her eyes, she shook her head. "You're going to need several stitches to close this."

He tried to pull his hand from hers. "I'll just wash it out with some peroxide and wrap it in gauze."

"No, you're not. You're going to the doctor."

"Am not."

"Yes, you are."

When their gazes locked, he couldn't believe how good she looked to him or how much he'd missed seeing her. For the past week, he'd given her the space he knew she needed and managed to be out of the house each morning before she arrived to work in his office. He'd even postponed taking the rest of the herds to auction in order to give her the coming weekend off.

But standing here staring at her now, he decided that space be damned. He wanted nothing more than to take her in his arms and kiss her until they both needed oxygen.

"Here's the first-aid kit," Greta said as she hurried down the hall. She stopped beside Cheyenne, took one look at his hand, then shook her head. "That's going to need more than anything we can do for you."

"He needs to see a doctor," Cheyenne said stubbornly.

"I couldn't agree more." Greta frowned. "Have you had a tetanus shot lately?"

Nick nodded. "About fifteen years ago."

"You're definitely going to the clinic," Cheyenne said, glaring at him.

Nick cringed when he thought about the injection they'd have to give him to numb his hand in order to stitch the wound shut, as well as the inoculation. Apparently an aversion to needles ran in the family because he suddenly understood why Hunter had had problems passing out every time he saw one.

"I don't like doctors."

"That's tough. You're going." Cheyenne held out her hand. "Give me your truck keys."

"If I go—and I'm not saying that I am—I can drive myself," he said stubbornly. He liked having her fuss over him. But this seeing-a-doctor business was getting out of hand.

"Nick." The tone of her voice warned him that she meant business.

Reluctantly placing the key ring in her outstretched hand, he shook his head. "This is ridiculous."

"Come on, cowboy." She tugged him along by his shirtsleeve. "The ordeal will be over with before you know it."

* * *

Two hours later, as Cheyenne drove them back from the clinic in Elk Bluff, Nick finally began to relax. His encounter with the barbed wire hadn't damaged any of the tendons in his hand and he hadn't humiliated himself by passing out when the doctor brought out the biggest hypodermic needle he'd ever seen to numb his hand.

"Are you in pain?" Cheyenne asked, steering his truck onto the highway leading out of Elk Bluff.

The concern in her voice caused a warm feeling to fill his chest. "Nope. In fact, I can't even feel my hand."

She smiled. "Just wait until the anesthetic wears off. I'm betting you'll feel plenty."

"Well, aren't you just a bright little ray of sunshine?" he said, tempering his sarcasm with a wide grin.

She laughed. "Seriously, you should probably take a couple of days off from working around the ranch to keep from tearing the stitches loose."

"I was thinking I might go down to Colorado this weekend to check out a free-range operation, then drive on to Albuquerque and spend some time there, so that won't be a problem."

"Oh." Pausing, she added, "I…hope you have a good time."

"I'm sure I will." Nick could tell Cheyenne was

curious about where he was going and who he'd be with, but she wasn't going to ask. "I'm going to help a relative celebrate *his* birthday."

"I didn't know that you had family down that way." Was that relief he heard in her voice?

He smiled. "Until just recently, I didn't know about it, either."

"It must be nice to have an extended family," she said, sounding wistful.

"Didn't your mother have a sister down in Laramie?" he asked, thinking back on what she'd told him about her mother.

She nodded as they drove up the lane leading to his house. "Yes, but we lost touch after a while and I haven't heard from her in years."

When she parked his truck and they went into the house, he motioned for her to follow him into the office. Picking up the envelope he'd received the day before from the Emerald, Inc. offices in Wichita, he pulled out a bank draft.

"I guess this answers our question about who you work for." Handing her the paycheck, he added, "But since I won't be here and there isn't any stock to tend, I'm giving you the weekend off."

Her fingers brushed his when she reached for the check and a charge of electric current streaked up his arm, then spread throughout his chest. Without thinking twice, he stepped forward and loosely wrapped his arms around her waist.

"Nick, I—"

"Shh. I'm not pressuring you to do something you can't or don't want to do." He lightly touched his lips to hers. "I just want to give you something to think about while I'm gone."

To his satisfaction as he settled his mouth over hers, Cheyenne melted against him and returned his kiss with a hunger that matched his own. Her sweet taste and the feel of her delicate frame pressed to him from shoulders to knees had the blood rushing through his veins and his body aching to claim her, to make her his once and for all. But he'd made her a promise and even if it killed him, he was going to prove to her that she could trust him.

After the confrontation with her father, then their talk on the way back from the auction, he'd decided she wasn't the only one who needed the space to think over a few things. In the past week, he'd done quite a bit of soul-searching on his own and reached several conclusions. Whatever genes he'd inherited from his irresponsible playboy father, the "love 'em and leave 'em" gene wasn't one of them. And although he'd fought with everything he had in him not to fall for Cheyenne again, he knew now that he'd never really had a choice in the matter.

She was his obsession—an addiction for him from which there was no cure. He'd pledged his love to her thirteen years ago and he knew now that was why he'd been unsuccessful at sustaining a relationship with anyone else. His heart had belonged and always would belong to Cheyenne. And whether she realized it or not, she felt the same way about him.

Breaking the kiss, he smiled as he stared into her beautiful aqua-green eyes. "While I'm gone, I want you to do something for me."

"Wh-what?"

He touched her satiny cheek with his finger. "I want you to think about us. I want you to think about me and how I make you feel. When I get back, we'll talk, sweetheart."

As the gray light of dawn began to chase away the dark shadows in her bedroom, Cheyenne lay in bed staring at the ceiling. She'd spent the entire night thinking about what Nick had said yesterday afternoon when he'd kissed her.

Didn't he realize he'd been all she could think about since finding him making repairs to that fence three weeks ago? Wasn't he aware that when he kissed her, nothing else seemed to matter but that she was in his arms? Or that when he made love to her she lost all sense of herself?

She scrunched her eyes shut to stop the wave of tears threatening to overtake her. She loved him— had never stopped loving him. But he'd made it clear that he didn't want her love and had no intention of returning it. And even if Nick did love her, she wasn't sure she could trust him.

He'd told her so many things about her father that she still had a hard time believing were true. Unfortunately, as much as she'd like to dismiss his accusations, she couldn't.

At the time, her father had been a powerful county judge with an intense dislike for Nick's family. And even though her father had always shown her nothing but love and kindness, she knew that he wasn't the same with others. His reputation of being very rigid and intolerant was legendary. But surely he wouldn't have misused his power to try ruining Nick's life, simply because Nick had tried to marry her.

She'd thought about confronting her father with Nick's accusations, but his blood pressure had been running a little high ever since they'd met up with Nick at the bar and grill. The last thing she wanted to do was run the risk of exacerbating her father's health problems with her questions.

"Cheyenne!"

The sound of her father's voice coming over the intercom system she'd had installed after his stroke caused her to sit straight up in bed. It wasn't unusual for him to rise around dawn each morning, but from the panic in his voice, she could tell something was terribly wrong.

She depressed the talk button on the unit beside her bed. "I'll be right there, Daddy."

"Hurry! The barn is on fire."

Cheyenne's heart pounded and her mind raced as she ran down the stairs. How many animals were in the barn?

The calves she'd isolated a few weeks ago had already been turned back into the herd after she'd successfully treated them for pink eye. But her gelding and Mr. Nibbles were still in the barn.

"Call the county fire department," she ordered as she ran past her father for the back door.

Sprinting down the wheelchair ramp and across the backyard, she ignored the pain of pebbles bruising the bottom of her bare feet as she crossed the gravel driveway. A chill snaked up her spine at the eerie glow she saw illuminating the otherwise dark interior of the barn and she was thankful that in deference to the August heat she'd worn a pair of gym shorts and a tank top to bed the night before. She had to get her gelding and the pony out of there and she didn't need the added encumbrance of her nightgown tangling around her legs.

"I called Gordon," he shouted as he wheeled his chair out into the yard after her. "He's contacting the county's volunteer firefighters."

"They'll never get here in time," she said, running toward the barn entrance.

"Cheyenne, no!"

Her father's panicked voice caused her to pause momentarily, but she continued on. Two animals were depending on her to lead them out safely and she wasn't going to let them down.

Nine

As the sky began to lighten, Nick steered his truck onto the road leading back to the Sugar Creek ranch. He'd left way before daylight to make the drive down to the free-range cattle ranch he'd heard about in Colorado. But the more miles he put between him and Cheyenne, the more he realized that leaving her behind was the last thing he wanted to do. They'd already spent thirteen years apart and as far as he was concerned, one more minute away from her was too damned long.

He had every intention of driving over to the Flying H later in the day, telling her father to get over whatever it was the man had against him and ask

Cheyenne to take a trip with him back to that little church across the county line. Only this time the outcome would be different. Come hell or high water, he was going to make her his wife.

Nick glanced toward the Holbrook place as he drove past and uttered a phrase he reserved for dire circumstances and smashed thumbs. Smoke billowed from the barn's hayloft and flames were visible along the outside wall.

Turning the truck around, he sped up the driveway to come to a sliding halt in the loose gravel. As he jumped from the truck, the sight of Cheyenne running into the burning barn caused fear to grip his insides and his heart to stall.

Bertram Holbrook jumped from his wheelchair surprisingly well for a man who was supposed to be partially paralyzed and began waving frantically toward the barn. "Get her out of there!"

Without thinking twice, Nick ran into the barn after Cheyenne. Catching her around the waist from behind, he spun her around and started pulling her toward the door. "What the hell do you think you're doing?"

She squirmed free of his grasp. "I have to get my horse and the pony."

"You get out of here. I'll get them," he shouted above the crackle of the rapidly spreading flames. "Which stalls are they in?"

She shook her head. "I'll get one while you get the other." Before he could stop her, she ran down the center aisle toward the fire.

Following her, Nick threw open a half door on one of the stalls and took hold of the halter on a fat, little chestnut pony. As he tugged the frightened animal along, he stopped at the stall where Cheyenne tried to catch a large buckskin gelding.

"Take the pony and go out the side door," he yelled, pushing her aside to keep the terrified horse from trampling her as it moved nervously around the stall.

When he grabbed the gelding's halter, Nick felt a sharp pain shoot up his arm as the stitches in his hand broke free, but he did his best to ignore it. Then, leading the panicked animal out into the center aisle, he fought to breathe as the choking smoke swirled around him and the terrified horse.

A loud cracking sound from somewhere overhead caused the gelding to shy away from him and Nick had to use every ounce of strength he possessed to bring the animal under control. Praying that Cheyenne and the pony had already made it to safety, he hurried to get himself and the buckskin out of the burning structure before the loft came crashing down on top of them.

He immediately released his hold on the gelding and let the horse run free when they reached the side

door of the barn and the safety of the outside. Looking around for Cheyenne, relief washed over him
when he spotted her several yards away. He started
toward her, but he'd only gone a few feet when the
sudden throbbing pain in his hand threatened to
buckle his knees. He stumbled and might have fallen
had she not rushed over to help steady him, and together they moved away from the burning building.

"Are you...all right?" he asked between fits of
coughing.

She nodded, tears streaming down her face as she
wrapped her arms around his waist and pressed herself to him. "I was so frightened that I might lose you."

His chest tightened with emotion and forgetting
all about his hand, he held her close. "Why were you
frightened, sweetheart?" He had a feeling he knew
the answer, but he wanted to hear her say the words.

"Because I—"

Her answer was cut short when a heavy hand
came down on Nick's shoulder. "There's no way
you're getting out of this one, Daniels. I've got the
evidence to prove your guilt this time."

Releasing her, Nick turned to face his assailant.
"What the hell are you talking about, Sheriff?"

The potbellied lawman waved a leather glove in
front of him. "This is yours, isn't it?"

Nick nodded as he stared at his missing work

glove. It would take a blind man or a fool not to see that he was being set up. Again.

"I thought as much," Sheriff Turner said, looking smug.

"Where did you find it?" Nick asked calmly. The sheriff had to have taken it from his truck the day he'd questioned Nick about the vandalism to Cheyenne's tires.

"It doesn't matter. It was found on the judge's property and you've already admitted it's yours." The man shook his head. "You should've stuck to misdemeanors. Arson is a felony and mark my words, you'll do time over this."

"Nick didn't set the fire," Cheyenne said, shaking her head.

Sheriff Turner shrugged. "I have proof that says otherwise. Besides, Daniels here left his ranch over an hour ago, then conveniently showed up here to help with the fire."

Nick gritted his teeth as he stared at the sorriest excuse for an officer of the law he'd ever seen. "How would you know that, unless you were watching my place, Sheriff?"

"I was out on patrol," the sheriff said, sounding a little less sure of himself.

"Before daylight?" Cheyenne shook her head. "You have deputies for that."

A dull flush began to spread over the man's face. "Now listen here, little girl—"

"Give it up, Gordon. It's over."

"Bertram, I've got Daniels right where we want him," Sheriff Turner said, reaching for the handcuffs clipped to the back of his belt.

Cheyenne turned to see her father coming toward them. He walked with a limp, but it was nothing that would keep him confined to a wheelchair. Nor were his movements and balance those of a man who was unpracticed at walking.

She felt the blood drain from her face as reality slammed into her like a physical blow. If her father had deceived her about his disability, he was certainly capable of everything Nick had alleged happened all the years ago.

As if sensing that she needed his strength, Nick put his arm around her shoulders. His silent support caused emotion to clog her throat.

"Why...Daddy?" Cheyenne asked brokenly. "How could you...be part of something...like this?"

For the first time in her life, she watched her father's shoulders sag and a look of utter shame to cross his face. "I—"

"Watch what you say, Bertram," the sheriff warned.

"What's the matter, Turner?" Nick's arm tightened around her. "Are you afraid the judge will name you as his accomplice?"

"Keep it up, Daniels, and I'll add resisting arrest to the arson and trespassing charges."

"You're not going to do a damn thing." Releasing Cheyenne, Nick turned on the sheriff. "Before you and the judge hatched up your plan, you should have made sure whose property you were torching. I own the Flying H Ranch."

"You're talking crazy," Turner blustered. "This place has always belonged to the Holbrooks."

"That's where you're wrong, Sheriff." Cheyenne glanced at her father. "Would you like to tell him, or should I?"

Her father suddenly looked ten years older. "I lost the ranch right after I had the stroke. Daniels is the owner of the Flying H now."

"And if there are any charges made, I'll be the one making them," Nick said, his tone leaving no doubt in Cheyenne's mind that he meant business.

She felt as if her heart broke all over again at the thought of her father being arrested. But what he and the sheriff had tried to do to Nick was incorrigible and she couldn't blame him for wanting to make them pay for what they'd done.

Despite a cool morning breeze, sweat popped out

on the sheriff's florid face as he glanced at her father. "If I go down, I'm taking you with me, Bertram."

She watched Nick step to within inches of the man's face. "Because I know how much it would hurt Cheyenne to see her father arrested, I'm going to shoot you a deal, Sheriff. And if you're smart, you'll take it because it's the only way you're going to keep yours and the judge's asses out of jail."

Sheriff Turner nodded. "I'm listening."

Nick pointed toward the remnants of the blazing barn. "This is your last official investigation. You're going to go back to Elk Bluff and file a report that this fire was an accident. Then you're going to turn in your resignation as County Sheriff, effective immediately."

"Now, see here—"

"You'd better think about it, Turner," Nick interrupted. "I've heard that lawmen and judges don't fare too well behind prison walls."

Cheyenne swallowed around the huge lump in her throat. She'd never loved Nick more. Even after all that her father and the sheriff had done to discredit him and set him up to face criminal charges—not once, but twice—he was willing to drop the matter in order to keep from hurting her.

"I think you'd better go, Mr. Turner," she advised the suddenly subdued sheriff. The sound of a distant siren grew closer. "That should be the county's volunteer fire department. I think they can take care of what's left of the barn, while you fill out that accident report and draft your resignation."

As the portly sheriff slunk back to his patrol car, Cheyenne turned to her father. "Let's go into the house for privacy. You owe Nick and me an explanation."

As Nick sat across the table from the judge in the Holbrook's kitchen, his hand throbbed unmercifully. But he wasn't going to drive down to the clinic in Elk Bluff to have the wound repaired until he had answers to the questions that had haunted him his entire adult life.

Before he could ask what the man had against him, Cheyenne must have noticed the fresh blood soaking through the bandage on his hand. "Oh, Nick, you've torn the stitches loose. You need to see the doctor."

He shook his head. "Not until I hear what your father has to say."

She stared at him for several moments, then, taking a deep breath, turned her attention to the silent man sitting on the opposite side of the table. "Why, Daddy? What could Nick have possibly done to you to deserve the way you've treated him?"

The tremor in her voice and the disillusionment in her eyes caused Nick's gut to twist into a painful knot. He felt her emotional pain all the way to his soul and he vowed right then and there that even if it killed him, he would never allow anything to hurt her again.

"I never meant for it to go this far," the judge said, sounding tired. Nick noticed that he kept his head lowered and couldn't quite meet their questioning gazes. "I only wanted to make you look bad. I never wanted anyone to get hurt."

"You're lucky no one did." Nick shook his head. "I think I lost ten years off my life when I saw Cheyenne run into that burning barn."

For the first time since Nick arrived, Bertram Holbrook looked him square in the eye, and for once there was no trace of animosity in the man's steady gaze. "I can't thank you enough for getting her out of there, Daniels. I don't know what I would've done if you hadn't shown up."

"Who set the fire—you or the sheriff?" Cheyenne asked.

"Gordon. But it wasn't supposed to get out of hand." The judge stared at his loosely clasped hands on top of the table. "It was supposed to be minor like the tire incident."

"That still doesn't answer my question. What do you have against Nick, Daddy? Why have you always despised him and his mother?"

The judge was silent for several long moments before he raised his head to look at Nick. "There was a time in my life that I wanted nothing more than to marry your mother. She was my high school sweetheart and I had it all planned out. After I finished college and law school, I was going to marry Linda, practice law and raise a family."

Shocked, Nick searched his memory, but he could never remember his mother mentioning that she and Bertram Holbrook had ever been anything but acquaintances. But before he could find his voice to ask the judge what happened between them, the man went on with his story.

"It all might have worked out, too, if she hadn't made that week-long shopping trip to Denver." The old man tiredly shook his head. "That's when I lost her. Once she met your daddy, she didn't want anyone else. I even offered to marry her and raise you as my own child after that philandering bastard left her alone and pregnant. But she wouldn't hear of it. She never would tell me the name of the man who stole her heart, but I hated him just the same. And I'm ashamed to say that hatred carried over to you."

"But what about Mama?" There was a tremor in Cheyenne's voice that tightened the knot in Nick's gut. "Didn't you love her?"

A lone tear spilled from Holbrook's eye. "Yes, princess. I loved your mother very much."

Tears streamed down Cheyenne's face and Nick moved his chair closer to hers and put his arm around her shoulders. "Then why did you—"

"Looking back over the way I've acted all these years…I'm not proud of it," the man said haltingly. "But I carried a grudge toward you and your mother, boy. And I couldn't stand the thought of you being with my precious daughter."

Nick wasn't sure what to say. For one thing, he was astounded that what little Bertram Holbrook had known about Nick's father was more than he'd known himself. There had been a time when he was young that he'd questioned his mother about who his father was and how she'd met him. But she'd only smile and tell him that the time would come when he'd learn about the man and why she didn't want to talk about him. After a while, he'd accepted her silence and stopped asking. He knew now that his mother's reluctance to talk about his father was due to the affidavit that Emerald had had her sign, requiring his mother's silence and ensuring that he would be an heir to the Larson fortune.

"That explains why you've treated Nick so poorly," Cheyenne sobbed. "But why have you deceived me all these years about your ability to walk? Didn't you know how heartbreaking it was for me to see my once strong father in a wheelchair?"

As Nick watched, Bertram Holbrook seemed to shrink before his eyes. "After I had the stroke I was afraid of losing you, princess. I know I've made a lot of enemies and I don't have many friends in this county." Nick almost felt sorry for the man when he reached for Cheyenne's hand and she moved it away from him. "You've always been the light of my life, princess. Since your mother died, you've been the only one to love me unconditionally and I was afraid of losing that." Tears ran unchecked down the judge's face. "But in my desperation to keep from dying a lonely old man, I only succeeded in driving you away."

"But you're my father. Didn't you realize that I would always love you? That I had enough room in my heart for you as well as Nick?"

Sensing that Cheyenne and her father needed time alone to sort through what was left of their father-daughter relationship, Nick kissed her temple, then rose to his feet. "I think the two of you need some privacy to work this out. I'm going to drive down to the clinic and have the stitches replaced in my hand."

Cheyenne looked torn between going with him and staying to work out things with her father.

Giving her a smile he hoped was encouraging, Nick walked to the door. "Come over to my place this afternoon and bring the copy of your contract. We need to settle a few things of our own, as well as dis-

cuss how all this is going to affect your employment
with the Sugar Creek Cattle Company."

By the time Cheyenne drove over to Nick's that
afternoon, she felt emotionally drained. After a long,
tearful discussion with her father, they'd come to an
understanding. He'd agreed to enter counseling to
help him deal with his propensity to manipulate
and control people and situations, as well as work
through his fears of being alone. And she was going
to make her own choices without his interference.

Parking her truck at the side of the Sugar Creek
ranch house, she took a deep breath and reached for
the file containing her contract on the seat beside her
as she readied herself for her meeting with Nick. She
knew he cared for her, but he'd made it clear there
was no chance of them having a relationship. And
they both knew that made it impossible for her to
continue working as the Sugar Creek foreman.

Before he fired her, she was going to do the only
thing she could do. She was going to turn in her resignation, move away from the area and find another
job to pay back the balance of her debt to Emerald, Inc.

When she got out of the truck and climbed the
porch steps, Nick opened the door before she had a
chance to knock. "You're late," he said as he took her
in his arms, then kissed her until she gasped for breath.

"I…didn't realize you'd set a time for this meeting."

"I didn't."

His hand at the small of her back as he guided her toward his office burned through her clothing and sent a shaft of longing straight to her soul. "Then why did you—"

"Because we've wasted enough time getting things settled between us." He reached for the folder in her hand, then tore it in half. "As of right now, you're no longer my employee or Emerald, Inc.'s."

She opened her mouth to tell him that he couldn't fire her because she was quitting, but he didn't give her the chance.

"And if you're worried about paying back the debt—don't. I've already made arrangements with Emerald Larson."

She shook her head. "I don't want you paying my debts."

"We'll talk about that later." His sexy smile caused her heart to skip several beats. "Right now, we have more important things to discuss."

Backing away when he reached for her, she shook her head. "Nick, I can't do this. I can't continue a 'no-strings' affair with you."

To her surprise instead of being disappointed, he grinned. "That's not what I want from you, sweetheart."

Hope began to blossom deep inside of her, but she

ignored it. She couldn't allow herself to believe that he'd changed his mind.

"What do you want?"

He quickly stepped forward and taking her by the hand, led her over to his desk. Activating the speaker phone, he pushed the speed dial. "I want you to listen in on a phone call I'm about to make. But you have to promise not to say anything until I hang up. Would you do that for me?"

"Okay," she said slowly. She wasn't sure what she expected him to say, but listening in on his phone conversation wasn't it.

When she heard her father's voice on the other end of the line, she started to protest, but Nick held up his index finger to silence her. "Judge Holbrook, Nick Daniels here. I have something I need to ask you."

From the long pause, Cheyenne thought her father was going to hang up. "Go ahead," he finally said.

Nick gave her a smile that she thought would surely melt her bones. "Sir, we both know that you haven't changed your mind about me nor will you ever think that I'm good enough for your daughter. But there's one thing you and I have in common. We both love Cheyenne more than life itself. And if she'll have me, I'd like to make her my wife."

A happiness that she'd never dreamed would be hers again filled her body and soul. Nick didn't want them to continue their affair. He loved her and wanted to marry her.

"Are you asking for my permission?" Instead of the animosity she expected to hear in her father's voice, there was only quiet resignation.

"No, sir." Nick cupped her face with his hand as he stared into her eyes. "I don't need your permission to marry your daughter. Whether or not she agrees to be my wife is going to be her decision. What I want from you is your blessing. We both know how much that would mean to Cheyenne and I want whatever makes her happy."

Leaning forward, Cheyenne kissed his firm male lips. "I love you," she mouthed as they awaited her father's answer.

"You'd better be good to her," her father warned.

Nick's expression turned serious. "Judge Holbrook, you have my word that I'll spend every minute of every day for the rest of my life doing everything I can to make her happy."

There was a long pause, then her father said the words that filled her with such joy she could no longer hold back her tears. "If you're what Cheyenne wants, then I have no objections and I'll accept the marriage with no further protest."

"Thank you, sir. I swear, I'll never let either of you down." Ending the call, Nick brushed his lips over hers. "Cheyenne Holbrook, I love you. Will you do me the honor of becoming my wife?"

"Oh, Nick, I love you, too. So very much." She threw her arms around her shoulders and kissed him. "Yes, I'll marry you."

His kiss was filled with such passion, such love there was no doubt in her mind that he meant every word he'd said about making her happy for the rest of their lives.

When he raised his head, the smile on his handsome face held the promise of a lifetime of love and happiness. "I'd like to get married as soon as possible if that's all right with you, sweetheart. I think we've waited more than long enough to start our life together, don't you?"

She returned his smile. "I couldn't agree more."

"What are you doing next weekend?"

"I'm not sure, but aren't you supposed to go down to Albuquerque—" She stopped short. "Weren't you going to go down to Colorado today, then drive on to New Mexico for your relative's birthday?"

He shrugged. "I got as far as the Elk Bluff city limits before I turned around and headed back." The tenderness in his deep blue eyes stole her breath. "I was on my way back for you."

"You wanted me to meet your relatives?" she teased.

"Well, I do want you to meet both of my brothers, as well as get to know my grandmother better, but the reason I came back was to see if I could settle things with your father and ask you to marry me."

Surprised by his statement, she shook her head. "Whoa, cowboy. Brothers and a grandmother?"

Nodding, he explained, "It turns out my mother wasn't the only woman my father impregnated. My brother Hunter is a year older than I am and my brother Caleb is a year younger."

"How long have you known about them?" she asked, feeling envious. She'd always wanted siblings.

"About two months. I found out about them at the same time I learned Emerald Larson is my paternal grandmother."

"*The* Emerald Larson is your grandmother?" No wonder there was such confusion over who her employer was.

As he explained about Emerald's stipulations that the women tell no one who'd fathered their babies because she'd wanted them to grow up without the temptations that had corrupted their father, Cheyenne nodded. "I can understand that she was only trying to protect you and your brothers, but it would have been so nice for you to have all known each other sooner."

"We're getting acquainted now and finding that

we have a lot in common." He laughed. "We all wonder what our all-knowing grandmother is going to spring on us next. When she gave each of us a company to run, she told us we'd get no interference from her. But we're finding that the old gal still has a few surprises up her sleeve. And I have a feeling that in our case, she was doing a little matchmaking in the bargain."

"I'm glad she did," Cheyenne said honestly. She reached out and cupped his lean cheek with her palm. "It's taken thirteen years, but I'm finally going to marry the love of my life."

"I love you, sweetheart."

"And I love you, Nick Daniels. More than you'll ever know."

He kissed her until they both gasped for breath. "How big of a wedding do you want?"

"I think just family would be nice."

"That might be a problem." He gave her a sheepish grin. "Once Emerald gets wind of our getting married, she's going to jump right in and help. And believe me, sweetheart. She doesn't do anything on a small scale."

"Do you think she'd be content with a small wedding and a big reception?" Cheyenne asked hopefully.

Nick nodded. "As long as you put her in charge of planning it, I think she'll be fine."

Her mind reeled from everything that had happened in the past few hours. "I still can't believe this is finally going to happen."

"Believe it, sweetheart. Nothing is going to keep me from making you my wife."

Happier than she'd ever been, Cheyenne kissed the man she'd given her heart to so long ago. "I can't wait to start our life together."

Taking her by the hand, he led her toward the door. "I can't, either."

"Where are we going?"

His grin caused her entire body to tingle as he hurried her up the stairs and into his bedroom. "To start our life."

Epilogue

"**H**ave Cheyenne and the judge arrived yet?" Nick asked as he checked his watch.

"They just drove up." Hunter laughed. "I didn't think I'd ever see any man more impatient to get married than Caleb. But I swear, I think you have him beat, Nick."

"I've waited a long time to make Cheyenne my wife." Nick checked the pocket of his Western-cut suit. "Do you or Caleb have the ring?"

"And I thought I was nervous when Alyssa and I got married." Caleb laughed as he walked into the room. "If you'll remember, you gave me Cheyenne's wedding band when we got here."

A knock on the door signaled that the wedding was about to begin and, taking a deep breath, Nick smiled at his two best men. "I'll feel a lot better when that ring is on her finger and this is a done deal."

As he walked out of the room they'd used to wait for the ceremony to begin, Nick looked around at the interior of the church. Other than a fresh coat of paint on the walls and a different-colored carpet down the center aisle, it looked much the same as he remembered.

Once he and Cheyenne had gotten around to talking about where to get married, they'd both agreed that the obvious choice for the wedding was the little church where they'd tried to become husband and wife thirteen years ago. But this time things were different. This time, instead of leading her away in tears, her father was going to walk her down the aisle and place her hand in Nick's.

When Nick took his place beside the minister and looked at the handful of people sitting in the pews, his grandmother caught his eye. At first, Emerald had been disappointed that the wedding was going to be limited to family. But when she heard they were turning the reception over to her, she was like a little kid at Christmas. And Nick had no doubt that she'd made poor old Luther Freemont's life a living hell when she made him the liaison between her and the people she'd hired to pull it all together on such short notice.

As the organist began playing "Here Comes the Bride," he turned his attention to the back of the church and watched as the double doors opened and Judge Holbrook escorted Cheyenne down the aisle. When they reached the altar where he stood with his brothers and the minister, Nick stepped forward and her father placed her hand in his.

The judge's eyes were suspiciously moist when he kissed Cheyenne's cheek, then turned to Nick. "Take good care of my princess, son."

As the judge limped over to sit on the front pew, Nick stared into the eyes of the most beautiful woman he'd ever seen. "I love you, Cheyenne. Are you ready for this?"

Her smile was filled with such love it robbed him of breath. "I love you, too, Nick, and I've been ready to become your wife for thirteen years."

"Then let's not wait a minute longer," he said as they turned to face the minister.

"And true love prevails," Emerald whispered as the handsome groom kissed his beautiful bride.

"Inevitably," Luther Freemont agreed.

Theirs hadn't been an easy journey, but in the end Nick and Cheyenne's love had won out and they were finally going to realize their dreams. Nick's idea to turn the Sugar Creek Cattle Company into a free-range cattle operation had been brilliant and Emerald had no doubt that it would be a huge success in the beef industry.

She turned her attention to Cheyenne. If her sources were correct, and Emerald had every reason to believe they were, she would be celebrating the birth of her first great-grandchild early next summer, right after Cheyenne graduated from college with a degree in elementary education.

More than happy with the results of her second matchmaking attempt, her gaze settled on her eldest grandson. Hunter was going to be her biggest challenge of all. His was a deeply wounded soul in need of healing. But she had every confidence that what she had planned for him would be just what he needed to come to terms with the past and move forward with his life.

As the minister introduced Nick and Cheyenne as Mr. and Mrs. Nick Daniels, Emerald leaned over to Luther. "Two down and one to go."

* * * * *

Don't miss
BETROTHED FOR THE BABY,
the next book in
Kathie DeNosky's
miniseries:
THE ILLEGITIMATE HEIRS.
Available March 2006 from
Silhouette Desire.

WHAT HAPPENS IN VEGAS...

Shock! Proud casino owner Hayden MacKenzie's former fiancée, who had left him at the altar for a cool one million dollars, was back in Sin City. It was time for the lovely Shelby Paxton to pay in full—starting with the wedding night they never had....

His Wedding-Night Wager

by **Katherine Garbera**

On sale February 2006 (SD #1708)

Also look for:

Her High-Stakes Affair, March 2006
Their Million-Dollar Night, April 2006

Silhouette Desire

Coming this March from

MARY LYNN BAXTER

Totally Texan

(Silhouette Desire #1713)

She's only in town for a few weeks...
certainly not enough time to start an
affair. But then she meets one totally
hot Texan male and all bets are off!

On sale March 2006!

![Silhouette®]

Desire®

THE ELLIOTTS

Mixing business with pleasure

The series continues with

Cause for Scandal

by
ANNA DePALO

(Silhouette Desire #1711)

She posed as her identical twin to meet a sexy rock star—but Summer Elliott certainly didn't expect to end up in bed with him. Now the scandal is about to hit the news and she has some explaining to do...to her prominent family and her lover.

On sale March 2006!

COMING NEXT MONTH

#1711 CAUSE FOR SCANDAL—Anna DePalo
The Elliotts
She posed as her identical twin and bedded a rock star—now the shocking truth is about to be revealed!

#1712 BETROTHED FOR THE BABY—Kathie DeNosky
The Illegitimate Heirs
What happens when coworkers playing husband and wife begin wishing they were betrothed for real?

#1713 TOTALLY TEXAN—Mary Lynn Baxter
He's the total Texan package and she's just looking for a little rest and relaxation…. Sounds perfect—until their hearts get involved.

#1714 HER HIGH-STAKES AFFAIR—Katherine Garbera
What Happens in Vegas…
An affair between them is forbidden, but all bets are off when passion strikes under the neon lights of Vegas!

#1715 A SPLENDID OBSESSION—Cathleen Galitz
She was back in town to get her life together…not fall for a man who dared her to be his inspiration.

#1716 SECRETS IN THE MARRIAGE BED—Nalini Singh
Will an unplanned pregnancy save a severed marriage and rekindle a love that's been stifled for five years?

SDCNM0206